THE HARVESTING

MELANIE KARSAK

CLOCKPUNK PRESS

Clockpunk Press, 2014
First edition: Steampunk Press 2012
Second edition: Clockpunk Press 2014
Copyright © 2012, 2014 Melanie Karsak
Published by Clockpunk Press
PO Box 560367
Rockledge, FL 32956-0367
www.clockpunkpress.com
Second edition cover art by Liliana Sanches
ISBN-10: 1479327247
ISBN-13: 978-1479327249

THE
HARVESTING

THE HARVESTING SERIES I

The world, it seemed, had gone silent. It was something we knew but did not talk about.
We were alone.

While Layla Petrovich returns home to rural Hamletville after a desperate call from her psychic grandmother, she never could have anticipated the horror of what Grandma Petrovich has foreseen. The residents of Hamletville will need Layla's cool head, fast blade and itchy trigger finger to survive the undead apocalypse that's upon them. But even that may not be enough. With mankind silenced, it soon becomes apparent that we were never alone. As the beings living on the fringe seek power, Layla must find a way to protect the ones she loves or all humanity may be lost.

ALSO BY MELANIE KARSAK

Forthcoming: Lady Macbeth; Wyrd Queen of
Scotland

THE HARVESTING SERIES:
The Harvesting
Forthcoming: The Shadow Aspect

THE AIRSHIP RACING CHRONICLES:
Chasing the Star Garden
Chasing the Green Fairy
Forthcoming: Chasing the Fog

for Erhan

CHAPTER 1

"IF YOU EVER NEED TO slice someone's head off, this is the blade you want," I said as I lifted a curved sword off the table in front of me. "We've been practicing épée and foil so far, but tonight I want to introduce you to the sabre." The practice sabre's curved blade reflected the orange streetlight shining in through the window. A grant from the Smithsonian where I worked allowed me to teach my two passions: ancient weapons and their arts. "The sabre is a slashing weapon," I continued and then lunged, showing the wide-eyed and excited students a few moves. "And in general, it's my favorite," I admitted with a grin.

The students laughed.

"Is that why you have it tattooed on your arm?" Tyler, one of my best fencers, asked.

My hand went unconsciously toward the tattoo. The ink was a sword interlaced with other once-meaningful symbols. "That's not just any sabre," I said, mildly embarrassed. "Here, let me show you. I brought something special tonight."

Setting the training sabre down, I lifted a rolled bundle. I laid it down on the table and unrolled it to reveal weapons in various elaborate scabbards.

"Some are épée, foils—you can tell by the hilt— a broadsword, a claymore, a katana, a scimitar, throwing daggers," I said, pointing, "but this, this is a Russian shashka." I pulled the shashka from the bundle. "It's like a traditional sabre, but has no guard. She's light, single-edged, wielded with one hand, and good for stabbing or slashing. Not awkward in close quarters like a Scottish claymore, but it will kill you just as dead," I said with a smile. I unsheathed the weapon and gave it an under-and over-hand spin around my head, shoulders, and back.

The students grinned from ear to ear.

I put it back in its scabbard and handed the shashka to them. "Pass it around, but keep in mind it is sharp enough to cut a blade of hair in half." I then turned my attention to Tyler. "Now, since you're so interested, let's see how you do with the sabre." I tossed one of the training swords to him.

Tyler, already in his gear, jumped up and lowered his fencing mask. "But you're not in gear," he said.

I shrugged. "Hit me, if you can."

We stood at the ready, made the ceremonial bow, and began. Tyler was not overly aggressive, which is partially why he was so successful. He waited for me, moving slowly. He was smart, quick, and often tried to over-tire his opponent.

I waited, dropped my sword a bit, and let him make the lunge. He took the bait.

The swords clanged together, and we clashed back and forth across the strip. He lunged and slashed while I dodged and blocked. He was fast. I was faster. When he lunged again, I ducked. With an upward movement, I went in.

"A hit," Kasey called.

They clapped.

"Man, that's what you get for taking on a former state champ—and the teacher," Trey told Tyler with a laugh.

Tyler pulled off the mask and smiled at me.

Just then, my cell rang. I would usually ignore it, but something told me to answer.

"Everyone pair up and start working with the training sabers," I said and pointed to the sword rack. I went to my bag and grabbed my cell.

Before I could say hello, she spoke.

"Layla, Grandma needs you to come home," my grandmother's voice, thick with Russian accent, came across through static. I was silent for a moment. My grandmother lived 500 miles away, and she never used her telephone. With the exception of her T.V., she hated technology. She'd cried and begged me to take away the microwave I'd purchased for her one Mother's Day.

"Grandma? What's wrong?"

"Come home now. Be here tomorrow," she said. She hung up.

I lowered my cell and stared at it. Confused and worried, I dialed her back. The phone rang, but she did not answer. I had obligations: practice, bills to pay, groceries to buy, tons of work to do, and a date for god-sakes. But my grandmother was the only one I had left in the world.

"Sorry, guys. Emergency," I called to my students.

Disappointed, they groaned.

"Sorry. Let's pack it up for the night." My hands shaking, I slid the shashka back into the bundle and rolled up the weapons. What had happened? Maybe Grandma was sick. Maybe she had some problem. Or maybe she had seen something.

The monuments on the Mall faded into the distance behind me as I made my way to my Georgetown apartment. It was Friday night. Wisconsin Avenue was packed. The upscale shops and restaurants teemed with people. In the crowd you could see the mix of international tourists, Georgetown students, and designer-dressed hotties headed to clubs. I sighed. For the last month I'd turned myself inside out trying to get the attention of Lars Burmeister, the German specialist the Smithsonian had brought in to consult on our new

4

medieval poleaxe exhibit. He had finally asked me to dinner; we were going to meet at Levantes, a Turkish restaurant near DuPont Circle, at nine that night. I had dreamed of authentic dolma and a chance to sit across from Lars somewhere other than a museum. I had even bought a new dress: black, strapless, come-hither.

I circled my block three times before I finally found a parking space. Regardless, I loved Georgetown. It was early fall. The mature trees had turned shades of deep red and orange and were losing their leaves. The air was filled with an interesting mixture of smells: the natural decay of autumn, dusty heat from the old cobblestone streets, and the mildly rancid odor of too many people. In my 4th floor attic apartment of an old Brownstone, I could occasionally catch the sweet scent of the Potomac River. It reminded me just enough of home.

The apartment was ghastly hot. The small, one bedroom place had been closed up all day. I lifted the window and let the noise of the city fill the room. The street lamps cast twinkling light across my apartment. The weapons I had mounted on the wall, swords, shields, axes and the like, glimmered. I peeled off my sweaty practice clothes. Pulling a bag from the closet, I threw in several changes of clothes and a few other supplies. On my coffee table, my laptop light blinked glaringly. An overflowing email inbox, an article on bucklers that needed editing for a peer-reviewed journal, and a PowerPoint on Medieval Russian swords for a presentation for next week's symposium all called me. My coffee table was stacked with paper. I was flooded with work; half my department was out on sick leave. There was a bad flu was going around. Thankfully, I had not yet gotten sick.

I pulled my cell out of my bag. I stared at the phone for a moment; Grandma's call was still displayed on the screen. I dialed Lars' number. My stomach shook when he answered.

"Guten abend, Lars. It's Layla."

"Ahh, Layla, good evening," he replied.

I loved his German accent. He'd learned English from a British teacher; he said arse with a German lilt. It made me smile. I could tell by his tone he was trying to hide his excitement. I didn't let him get far. I told him I had been called away for an emergency. I could sense his disappointment.

"I'll be back by Monday. Let me make it up to you. Dinner at my place Monday night?"

He agreed.

"Gute nacht," I said as sweetly as possible, hoping I had not pissed him off, and stuffed my phone into my bag. I stared out the window taking in the view. I didn't want to go back, not even for a weekend. I loved my life. Hamletville was an old, ghost-filled place: too many memories, too much heartache. Yet I knew my grandmother. If she said I needed to come home, then I needed to come home.

I closed the windows, slid on a pair of jeans, a black t-shirt, boots, and a light vest. I looked again at the display on the wall. At the center I had crossed two Russian poyasni or boot-daggers. One dagger had the head of a wolf on the hilt. The other had the head of a doe. I grabbed them and tossed them in my bag. I then headed back downstairs and into the night. It was the last time I would lay eyes on Washington.

CHAPTER 2

HAMLETVILLE. MY GRANDMOTHER HAD travelled from the Mother Country all alone. When she arrived in New York, she got on a westbound train and stayed on until "the spirits told me to get out at Hamletville, so I got out." She'd purchased as much land as her money could buy: 100 acres backed up to a National Forest. She said she felt safe there. While her profession was a seamstress, her true talent was as a Medium. And according to the children of Hamletville, she was also a witch.

My grandma, however, had done her best to raise me. When my mother ran off with the town drunk—and who knows who my father was—my grandmother had not batted an eyelash. She moved me into the Fox Hollow Road cabin and took care of me. My mother never came back.

I was sleepless, smelled like Doritos, and had drunk far too much bad coffee, but almost eight hours later my SUV rolled into the small town of Hamletville. It was like reliving a bad nightmare. Memories of an only occasionally happy childhood and even worse youth lived on every corner. When I drove past *his* shop, my heart still hurt—even four years later. I strained my neck to try to catch a glimpse. Nothing.

My Range Rover easily took the bumps, turns, holes, and trenches of Fox Hollow Road. Guilt overwhelmed me when I arrived. It had been almost a year since I'd been back. My grandmother's lawn had not been mowed in ages; weeds were knee high. Some shingles had come off the roof, and the place looked even more like a witches' cabin than ever. My grandmother had closed all the shutters on the house and had nailed boards across most of them. Despite the fact the sun had just risen, my grandmother was there, hammer in hand, working on barring up the front picture window. She was wearing a purple checked dress, and her hair was covered in an old yellow and blue flowered babushka. When she saw me, she came off the porch and waived my SUV forward.

My first thought was that she was not well. Last year my assistant's mother had entered early stages of dementia and started displaying odd behavior. Perhaps my grandmother . . .

"No, no, Layla, Grandma is fine. Come. Help me now," she said, interrupting my thoughts as she opened the door to my SUV. "Oh, Layla, you need a shower."

"Of course I do, Grandma. I just drove across four states to get here."

"Ehhh," she muttered then led me into the house.

The scene was one of complete disarray. It looked like she had unloaded every cupboard and was sorting items.

"Tomorrow the men come to fix the roof and clean the chimney. Already I've had wood delivered, but Layla, I had the men put it in the dining room. I know, everyone thinks Grandma is crazy."

"Well, Grandma, it is a dining room." I noticed that the old oak China cabinet had been pushed in front of the living room picture window. It blocked most of the light.

"Grandma . . ." I began, but I was not sure what to say.

"Here, Layla, I want you to go to the store. Buy all the things on my list. No questions. Just buy it all," she said then handed me a wad of hundred dollar bills. I looked from the money to the list to her and back to the list again. "No questions," she said, "but take a shower first. You stink."

"Grandma!"

"I'll get you a towel."

My grandmother's bathroom, decorated with red lace trimmed towels and smelling like lemons, was a stark contrast to the rest of the house. So confused by the scene, I didn't know what to do. Like the obedient girl I'd always been, I did what she told me. As the water poured over me, I tried to make sense of what was going on. All I knew was every hair on the back of my neck had risen and there seemed to be an odd buzzing in my ears, like the feeling of being near something high voltage. I tried to shake it but couldn't. My grandmother's seriousness made me want to obey her, but too much life and education made me want to stop in my tracks.

When I came out of the shower my grandmother was nowhere to be found. She'd left me a clean towel and a note written in Russian: "Went to the woods. Will be back. You go to the store."

I went to my room to unpack. It was full of boxes. Inside I found cases of antibiotics, bandages, and other medical equipment. I dressed quickly and went onto the front porch. From that vantage point, I noticed that Grandma had recently installed a very tall chain-link fence around the house. I was so tired when I'd arrived I hadn't notice it. The gate stood ajar. Grandma must have left it open when she went on her walk. Things were getting weirder by the moment.

"Grandma?" I called into the forest behind her house, but there was no reply. I decided to head to town.

It was a Saturday morning, and the streets of the sleepy town were a-typically quiet. I pulled into the parking lot of *Hicktown Hardware and Huntin' Goods*. At least the owners, the Lewis family, had a sense of humor. I made a silent prayer to God that I wouldn't run into anyone I knew. No luck.

"Ah, Layla, are you here to pick up Grandma Petrovich's order?" the owner, Mrs. Lewis, asked as she snubbed out her cigarette. The air around the cash register was hazy blue. I had not seen Mrs. Lewis in almost five years, but she still looked exactly the same: tightly permed brown hair, overly thick, smoke-stained glasses, and blazing-pink fingernail polish. She'd been glued to a small T.V. sitting beside the cash register. I could hear the over-expressive voices of excited newscasters.

I nodded. "She added a few more things," I said and read off the list which included more batteries than one person could need in a lifetime, two-way radios, three axes, and high-powered binoculars.

Mrs. Lewis instructed a shop boy to gather the items on my list. I paid cash, nearly $1200, for all of the items, including the preorder which was packed into mystery boxes.

At the grocery store I was met with a similar preorder.

"Have to admit," Clark said as he helped me load my SUV, "I was surprised to hear your

Grandma on the phone. She is almost a recluse. I think Father Meyers checks in on her from time to time, but otherwise she doesn't come out much anymore. What is she doing with all this stuff anyway?"

Something inside me told me to lie. "We're going on a trip out west. You know how these old people are. She wanted to make sure we had enough."

"You gonna rent an RV or something?"

"Yeah, that's the plan."

"Whoa, what are these?" Clark asked as he stumbled across the swords and fencing gear I had left in the back.

"Swords, actually. Well, I should be getting back," I said, looking down at Grandma's list. Clark waved goodbye, and I slid back into my SUV. The first two stops on the list were not difficult, but the next two puzzled me.

She left instructions for me to stop by *Campbell Feed and Lumber*. She knew very well that was the last place I would go. She wanted fifty pound sacks of corn and wheat flour. I looked up the street toward the shop. I waited. After a few moments, Ian appeared on the loading dock outside the store. He lowered two large bags onto the back of a flatbed pickup. He laughed as he talked to the driver. I could almost see that funny wrinkle he gets in the corner of his mouth when he smiles. He waved goodbye to his customer and turned to go back inside but then he stopped. He looked up the street, his eyes settling on my SUV. He took two steps down the loading platform toward me.

"Oh my god," I whispered.

A moment later, Kristie, his wife, appeared at the shop door and called him back inside. He turned, casting one last look my way, then went in.

"Bitch," I whispered and turned the ignition over in my car and headed up Lakeview Drive toward the Catholic Church.

My grandmother was not a religious person. Whenever she was invited to go to church, she would decline, saying "no, no, no, I am Russian Orthodox," and the conversation would end. Privately, however, I had never seen my grandma act in any way that was remotely Christian. In fact, some of her odd "old country" practices often had a pagan flavor.

When I got to the Catholic Church the doors were open. I stopped when I entered, taking a moment to smooth my hair, checking my reflection in a mirror hanging on the wall just by the door. I was glad Grandma had made me take a shower. I pulled my thick black hair into a ponytail. The church candlelight made my green eyes sparkle.

"Can I help you?" a voice asked.

I turned to see Father Meyers standing there. It had been years since I'd last seen him. He used to coach the boys high school basketball team. He looked so much older. "Father, I'm Layla Petrovich. My grandmother asked me to come see you," I replied.

"Ah yes, Layla. How is your grandmother?" He was quick to hide his confusion. I could almost hear him thinking: *what is she doing here?*

"I'm not sure, Father. But, regardless, my grandmother asked me to come by and request holy water."

"Whatever for?"

"To be honest, I don't know. My grandmother has her ways, and most of the time I just do what she wants."

Father Meyers laughed. "Well, with Grandma Petrovich, I understand. Now, we are not in the practice of giving out holy water, but I suppose it won't hurt anything. I'll be back in a moment," he said and went to the rectory.

I sat in the last pew and waited. I felt like a stranger in a strange land. The stained glass windows bore images of saints. The window closest to the pew where I sat had an image of St. Michael slaying a dragon. Behind me a statue of Mary stood over the votive prayer candles. Five candles were lit. Their flames cast glowing light on Mary's elongated face and hands. The statue depicted Mary with overly-white skin and pale lips. She wore the lightest of blue robes. A small chip had come off one side of her nose, disfiguring her. It showed the gray plaster beneath. I closed my eyes. The images in the church bombarded me. I could not quiet my mind. Flashes appeared before my eyes, random unclear images. Then the face of a dead woman appeared before me; like Mary, her nose was torn off. She was grunting and biting at me through a fence. Though her decayed face was horrific, I noticed she had a striking red ribbon in her hair. I shuddered, my eyes popping open.

"Here you are, Layla. Can I expect you and Grandma at Mass this Sunday?"

"Thank you so much, Father. I appreciate it. No, I'm sorry. You know we are Russian Orthodox. Thank you again," I said and hurriedly left the church.

Before heading back to my SUV, I walked to the cemetery to the right of the church. Grandpa Petrovich was buried there. It occurred to me that Grandma might not have been by to clean his headstone. I walked toward the tall willow tree; Grandpa Petrovich was buried underneath.

Though I had never met him, I'd heard about Grandpa Petrovich often enough that he seemed alive in my memory. My grandma loved to tell their story. Back in Russia, their families had known one another. They courted but nothing came of it. Then my grandmother decided to come to the US. My grandfather, Sasha, had written to her every week for five years asking her to come home. Since she always refused, he finally came to the US to join her. They were married almost immediately, and my mother was conceived. But my grandfather died shortly after coming to the United States. There had been some sort of accident at his work. "Well, I told him not to come," my grandmother would say, but I saw the pain behind her eyes. I always wondered if she had foreseen his early death.

I found his monument in the same state as Grandma's house. First, I cleared away the weeds. Taking a scarf from my pocket, I wiped off the face of his tombstone. It was a shame. I would bring my grandmother by to plant some flowers.

"Layla, is that you?" someone called.

I turned to find Ethel, my classmate Summer's mother, crossing the cemetery. She was carrying a basket. Inside I saw she had stashed a small shovel and gloves.

I rose, wiping my hands on my jeans. "Hey Ethel," I called and walked to join her.

She mopped sweat from her brow. "How long you in town for?"

"Not sure, actually."

"I'll tell Summer you're home. How is Grandma Petrovich?"

Indeed, how was she? "About the same."

Ethel smiled knowingly. How many times had Ethel sat across the kitchen table from my grandma

17

to hear advice from the spirit world? "Well, your Grandma always tells it like it is, but I sure was glad she was there when your mother ran off. You ever hear anything from her?"

I shook my head. "For all I know she's dead."

Ethel sighed. "That is a pity. She'd be really proud of you, honey. You had a rough start, but you sure made good out of it. Of course you were always the smartest child I ever saw. No one was surprised when you got that scholarship, but I think most people worried that Campbell boy would--"

"Planting flowers on Phillip's grave?" I interrupted. Ethel's husband had died the year Summer and I were juniors.

We looked across the graveyard together. "Oh, yes, every fall I plant chrysanthemums," Ethel said. "Seems like they've buried a lot of folks the last couple of weeks," she added and pointed to some freshly dug graves.

We turned and walked back toward the street.

"Some kind of bad flu going around," Ethel said as we walked by one of the fresh graves. "We lost old Mrs. Winchester," she added, pointing to the grave nearest us. "You know she had a green burial? They dropped her in the ground wrapped in nothing but a light blue shroud. Oddest thing. "

We stared down at her grave.

"I loved her oatmeal cookies," I said.

Ethel looked questioningly at me.

The soil stirred.

"Watch yourself, Layla. The earth is still settling," Ethel said, pulling me back and looping her arm in mine.

I walked Ethel to her car. She opened the trunk and dropped the basket inside. She then turned and hugged me. "Don't be a stranger, honey. Come by and see us," she said, squeezing my arm, then she got into her car. With a wave, she drove off.

I gazed toward the graveyard. Mrs. Winchester had been the town librarian. I used to sit in the back of the library and hide from my mother, hide from whatever man she'd dragged home that week, hide from the chaos of our house. Mrs. Winchester would give me homemade oatmeal cookies and would lie to my mother when she came looking for me. Mrs. Winchester would wait for my grandmother to turn up. From time to time I still craved those cookies. As I slid back into my SUV, I made a mental note to pick up some flowers for Mrs. Winchester too.

When I got back to the cabin it took nearly an hour to unload all of Grandma's supplies. By the time I had finished, Grandma returned from her walk.

"Ah, Layla, my good girl. Thank you so much," Grandma said and clasped her hands together.

I noticed she was carrying her herb satchel. "Harvesting, Grandma?"

She laughed. There was a hard edge to it. "Oh, yes, it is harvest season. Come. Now we go in and get everything ready."

"Ready for what?"

"Ehh, you'll see. Come now, Layla."

That night Grandma and I turned the house upside down. Grandma must have tossed forty years of junk, knick-knacks, and all of the other useless things a person collects over a lifetime. In their place she stocked the cupboards with supplies. I must have made 10 trips to the dumpster at the end of Fox Hollow Road. No matter how many times or ways I asked why she had all that stuff or why she was throwing everything away or why she had called me or what was wrong, all Grandma would say is "you'll see." Thinking of all the possible answers she could have given, that one seemed the worst.

I woke near noon the next day to the sound of men hammering on the roof. Grandma was in the kitchen storing a massive tray of beef jerky.

"That looks like a whole cow," I said with a yawn as I sat down at the table.

"Two," she answered absently as she stopped her work to pour me a cup of coffee.

"Why two?" I asked as I stirred in the cream.

"The spirits said two, so I made two," she replied.

I stopped and looked at her. "Grandma?"

"Tu-tu-tu-tu," she jabbed at me with a wave of the hand. "I made you piroshky," she said, pulling the warm pastry from the oven. All other thoughts left my mind. "I love you, Grandma," I said with a laugh.

She chuckled. "My darling."

After I ate, Grandma put me to work. We boarded up the barn windows, secured loose hinges, stored food, and sharpened axes. We were adjusting the last items in the kitchen when Grandma asked: "Where is the flour?"

I pretended not to hear.

"Layla?"

"I couldn't do it."

"Oh, my Layla, that boy, he is so stupid. He had a beautiful Russian girl like you, and he married that stupid fat girl with a face like a donkey. And for what? She didn't even carry that baby to term. You see, she just got that baby to steal that boy from you, and now he is stuck with her. He is too stupid, Layla. And thanks to him, now you have that ugly tattoo on your arm and shoulder. What about some nice rich man? Didn't you find a nice man at the Smithsonian? So many nice looking men in suits in Washington, so many soldiers . . ."

She continued, but I'd tuned her out. She was right. Ian was stupid. After one fight, Ian had slept with someone else. His dumb, rash decision resulted in the conception of an innocent child who, sadly, had not lived. Ian had done right by Kristie and married her, but he had not done right by me.

". . . and anyway, it no matter. Come tomorrow, no one will care anymore anyway. You see, all things happen for a reason. Now, we are done here. I will go pay the men for the roof, then I will show you the guns, then we'll drink tea."

"Guns?"

"Ehh, peel some potatoes," she then wandered outside, still muttering.

CHAPTER 3

"THIS IS A GLOCK 17 SEMI-AUTOMATIC pistol. Most policemen use this gun. Comes with 17 rounds. You pop in the cartridge like this and . . ." Grandma squeezed the trigger, blasting a decorative plate with a picture of fruit on it. It used to hang in the dining room. Ignoring my astonished impression, she handed the gun to me. "Didn't you go hunting with the Campbells?"

"Yes. I can shoot a gun, Grandma," I said bewildered. Why in the hell did my grandmother have a semi-automatic pistol? We were standing behind the barn. She had guns laid out on the lid of an old feed barrel. I set the gun down.

"Good, good, then you'll have no problem. Now, this is .44 Magnum, like the *Dirty Harry* movie. It has good stopping power. Lift up the safety and boom," Grandma said pulling the trigger. The gun barrel let out a resounding noise, shattering Grandma's old mantle-piece vase. "The man told Grandma this is a kill-shot gun, very powerful," she said and set the gun down.

I picked it up, took aim at an old porcelain figurine, and fired. The smiling cherub exploded into a puff of dust.

"Very good! Ahh, here we are," she said picking up what looked like a machine gun. "This is Colt 9mm sub-machine gun. Grandma had a hard time getting this one, but a nice man on the phone, of course he was Russian, helped Grandma get this one ordered for you. This gun can shoot almost 1000 rounds per minute. Very fast, no?" Grandma said and launched a spray of bullets toward the remaining china pieces she had set up on the fence-post. "Here, you try. Watch for kick back," she said and handed the gun to me.

I set the gun down and took Grandma by the hands. "Grandma, what in the hell is going on? You're scaring me."

"Shoot first," she said, picking the Colt back up and handing it to me.

I sighed. The gun, surprisingly, didn't feel heavy in my hands. I held it as I had observed Grandma doing, and as every drug smuggler on T.V. had done, and let off an easy rattle of ammo.

"You see, very easy."

I set the gun back down. "That is enough, Grandma. Please. What is happening?"

Grandma inhaled deeply and took me by the chin. She looked into my eyes then kissed me on both cheeks. "First, we'll put guns away," she said, picking up the weapons. "Oh, I also bought grenades. Just like on T.V.: pull the pin, throw, it explodes."

"Grenades?"

After we had restocked Grandma's personal arsenal, we went back inside.

"Sit down in living room. Watch T.V. I'll make tea," she said and wandered into the kitchen.

"But Grandma—"

"Tu-tu-tu," she said to shush me. "You watch T.V. I'll come in a minute."

I flipped on the T.V. to find it tuned to the news channel. At once I saw what appeared to be a riot taking place. At first it looked like just another scene of violence, but then I started reading the crawling banner: wide spread outbreak and rioting in major US cities in the south and on the west coast. Police had instituted martial law in LA, Miami, and Atlanta. Outbreak reports were cropping up in all major US and foreign cities. Airlines had closed all international travel. The United States President has been moved to a protected location.

The T.V. buzzed with three loud chimes: the Emergency Broadcast System had been activated. The screen went blue and after a few minutes, an official looking White House spokesman appeared at a podium, the emblem of the CDC hanging behind him.

"Grandma? You should come see this," I called to her. I felt like someone had poured cold water down my back. Every hair on the back of my neck was standing on its end. Is this what Grandma had foreseen? Is this why I was here? Did the spirits tell her something?

"At this point it appears to be a highly contagious flu-like pandemic," the Director of the CDC was saying.

"Citizens are urged to stay inside their homes. Military personnel have been dispatched to major US cities," the White House spokesman added.

A reporter asked why the pandemic seemed to happen almost overnight. I noticed then that the press were all wearing surgical masks.

"Incidents of flu have been steadily on the rise for the last one week which has exacerbated accurate diagnosis. The symptoms of this particular strain resemble seasonal flu at the onset—body pain, fever, and vomiting—but gradually worsen with additional non-normative symptoms," the Director of the CDC explained.

"Non-normative? What does that mean, and how is it being spread?" a female reporter asked. I recognized her from the President's regular Press Club. I'd seen her in person once at a downtown café. She'd been eating a massive plate of fries.

The Director of the CDC gave a sidelong look toward the White House spokesman. "Citizens should avoid direct physical contact with the sick until we can pinpoint the cause," the CDC Director said at last.

"Is there a vaccine or immunization?" another reporter asked.

"Until the cause is identified, it is difficult to develop a vaccine, but we are working around the clock analyzing possible contaminants," the Director replied.

"What is the mortality rate?" someone asked.

The Director of the CDC looked uncomfortable. "It is difficult to ascertain. At this point the mortality rate appears to be 100%, but post-mortem there appears to be brain activity-"

"No further questions at this time," the White House spokesperson said with a scowl and ushered the Director of the CDC out of the room.

Grandma sat down beside me, setting a serving tray on the coffee table. She picked up the remote and muted the T.V.

In the far off distance, we heard the alarm on the town fire hall wail. It was used to call in emergency volunteer firefighters and medical personnel or to warn of tornado. Three rings to call for help. Seven rings for tornado warning. The alarm wailed and did not stop.

"When I was 12 years old, my grandma knew I had the sight," my grandmother began. "My mother only had the gift a little. She had good instincts, but she never heard the spirits. I was lucky. I was born with the mark of the bear," she said, showing me the small birthmark on her knee shaped like a bear's paw, "so everyone knew I would have the gift. But when I was 12, my grandmother sat me down in her living room and poured me a cup of tea," she said as she poured me a cup. I noticed that she had placed two slices of a strange looking mushroom in the water. "My grandmother told me, while I was lucky to hear the spirits, there are other things in this world, some good, some evil. There exists spirits, demons, creatures who are not like us. She wanted me to see them. She wanted me to be safe from them. She said that until the great eye inside is awake, we do not see them. She said, I must awaken and see. That is what my grandmother told me as she handed me a cup of tea," my grandma said then handed the mushroom tea to me.

I took the cup. I looked back at the T.V. and saw strange images of people in hospital gowns being shot by military men.

"Drink," Grandma encouraged.

I did as she asked, polishing off the cup.

"My grandma loved me. She tried to protect me by making me see the otherworld. She was right. Afterward, I saw and heard spirits and those other things in this world. This has kept me away from evil and has helped me see good. Did you know there are forest spirits living right behind our house? Ehh, anyway, my grandmother loved me, so she made me see. I drank the tea then slept for almost two days. When I woke, I could see."

My head felt woozy. Images on the screen melted into a strange haze. I reached out for my grandmother.

"You sleep now. I'll go close the fence and bar up the doors. It has already begun," she said.

"What has begun?" I asked drunkenly. The room spun, and I felt like I might be sick.

"The harvest," she replied. I heard the front door open and close then everything went black.

CHAPTER 4

WHEN I WOKE, THE *zong, zong, zong* throbbing in my head felt like it would never stop. I'd once dragged Ian on a winery trail tour. I'd drunk my weight in Merlot and woke the next morning with a similar mix of sour mouth, blaring headache, and nauseous stomach. I could not believe my grandma had drugged me—oh wait, yes, I could.

The alarm on the fire hall had stopped blaring, but the bell on the Catholic Church was now clanging, making my head ache even worse. To top it off, I had just awoken from the strangest nightmare. In my dream, a robed figure invited me to join him at the harvest. Excited, I picked up a wicker vegetable basket and went with him. Much to my confusion, he led me to a graveyard. I asked him, "Why are we here?" The hooded figure turned toward me, showing me his skeletal face. He extended his boney arm, brandishing his sickle across the tombstone vista. "Why, we are here for the harvest," he said in reply. When I looked back, I saw the graveyard was on fire. I shuddered as I remembered his words.

"Grandma?" I called as my feet hit the hardwood floor. There was no reply.

I went to the living room to find the T.V. on, but the screen was buzzing static. I clicked it off. The smell of burning bacon assailed my nose. I went into the kitchen, which was full of smoke, and turned the heat off. I threw the pan, the bacon burned black, into the sink. It hit the water with a sizzle. I cracked the window to let the smoke out.

"Grandma?" I called again.

I poured myself a glass of water and checked the rest of the house. Grandma was nowhere to be found, but the radio in her room was on. The announcer was listing names of cities now under quarantine. He might as well have said the entire United States. My skin turned to goose bumps. What was happening?

I went back to the living room. The front door was unlocked and unbarred; apparently, Grandma had gone outside. My head aching, I slipped on a pair of jeans and t-shirt. There was a chill in the air, so I grabbed my vest, pulled on my hiking boots, and headed outside.

The driveway gate was closed but not locked. The church bell continued to ring. The sound was shrill. I couldn't find Grandma anywhere. Knowing her, she was in the woods digging up more mushrooms—we needed to have a serious talk about that. Strange she'd forgotten about the bacon.

I checked the barn. She wasn't there, but I spotted the binoculars I'd picked up at the hardware store. I grabbed them and headed to the back of the property. I scaled the fence and walked into the woods. A trail behind the cabin led in two directions; one direction led into the National Forest, and the other, if you scaled the mountain, led to the Point. The Point was the old Native American lookout on the mountaintop. It looked over the town and across the lake.

I climbed up the side of the hill. How many times had I fled to the woods and hiked to the Point? It was an escape. It was a peaceful place. I wound through the mountain laurel and over the mossy rocks up the side of the hill. The fallen autumn leaves, warm under the sun, provided the effervescence of decay. I felt the grainy grit of limestone and tree bark as I grabbed for handholds to pull myself upward. Finally, I got to the top of the hill. Now all I needed to do was scale the boulder that capped it. I had done it a hundred times. I knew every foot-and handhold. I pulled myself toward the top.

I was treated to a vista of autumn leaves: red, orange, and vibrant yellow. The cool wind whipped hard, blowing my hair around me. I looked toward town, but it was a long ways away. With the naked eye, I could easily make out the streets and rooftops. I could see people in the streets, but something seemed off. It looked like the Jamesons' house was on fire.

I pulled out the binoculars, making some minor adjustments, and looked down. The Jamesons' house *was* on fire and so was the flower shop next door. There were people all over the streets. Most of them were not moving. I could not see their faces clearly, but they looked sick. They were pale and bloody. I scanned over to the Catholic Church. The bell was still ringing. A few people stood outside looking at the building. The pandemic had come. How long had I slept?

Then I heard a popping sound. It was coming from the lower end of town. I scanned and saw a group of about fifteen people running toward the community building. They were shooting behind them. A horde of maybe twenty or thirty people followed them. They ran, shot, and ran more. Someone fell down. The horde behind swarmed over them, and I saw a flash of red blood. I nearly dropped the binoculars.

Again, gunshots rang out. Another group emerged from a side street. My heart sank. Ian was there; Kristie was beside him. Ian's older brother, Jamie, was with him, and so were Summer and Ethel. They joined the larger group, and they all headed toward the community center.

I sat down on the boulder. My senses were on edge. I could hear every bird and insect around me. My system, sensing danger, had gone into over-drive; yet, there was no danger near me. I was isolated. But Ian was in trouble. The group entered the community center, but a huge horde circled the place. Drawn by the sound of gunfire, the sick began to gather and claw at the windows and doors. The place was completely surrounded.

I lowered the binoculars. My hands felt ice-cold. A chilled wind whipped through me and a feeling like electricity filled the air.

"Help them," a male voice said from behind me.

I leapt up, nearly losing my balance and going over. I righted myself at the last moment. I found myself staring at and staring through the figure of a Native American chief in full ceremonial regalia. He was young, very handsome, and feathers and beads were braided into his long hair. He was clearly there and clearly transparent all at once. He knocked an arrow on his bow, and the illusory weapon shot toward town. I watched the arrow fly toward the community building then fade.

I turned back.

"Help them," he said again. Another strong wind swept through. Like he was made of sand, the chief's image blew away, disintegrating back into the wind, until nothing but the image of the bow remained. Then, it too faded, blowing back into the realm of the spirit.

CHAPTER 5

MY WHOLE BODY SHOOK AS I raced through the woods to the cabin. My mind was in a fit of fear and adrenaline. I clambered over the back fence and rounded the barn. I was about to call for my grandma when I saw Mr. and Mrs. Fletcher, whose farm was closest to our cabin, standing, just standing, in the driveway. The driveway gate was slightly ajar. I gasped and slid back behind the barn. I couldn't get to the house. I couldn't get into the barn. I checked my pockets. My car keys were there.

Quickly, I ran from the side of the barn to my SUV. The *beep beep* of my doors unlocking woke the Fletchers from their sick slumber. They both turned and lunged toward me. They were amazingly fast. I ran. I opened the back passenger door and jumped into the backseat. I slammed the door shut behind me, locking the doors with a thump. The Fletchers were at the SUV in moments.

They were sick or maybe even dead. Their skin was corpse white, and their eyes were cloudy white with red bloodshots striking through. Their mouths frothed, and they lunged, over and over, biting and snapping at me. Bloody saliva smeared across the black-tinted windows of the Range Rover.

I could feel my heart beating in my throat. I climbed over the backseat and into the cargo space. Suddenly, I touched something hard. My swords. Who says it doesn't pay to be a medievalist? I pulled the shashka from the bundle and strapped its scabbard around my waist. Then I unsheathed the weapon. I had to find my grandmother.

The Fletchers were flailing about at the passenger side window. I took a deep breath and opened the back. I slid out and headed toward the driver's side. The Fletchers moved toward the back of the SUV. Dropping low, I swung around the front of the car. They were at the back. I leaned down and watched their feet. I didn't know what to do, but I needed to do something fast.

I took a few deep breaths and turned toward the house. With the shashka poised in front of me, I kept one eye on the Fletchers as I backed toward the cabin. The moment they saw me, they closed in.

"Stay back!" I yelled, but they didn't seem to hear. They came toward me, grabbing at me, snapping while bloody saliva dripped from their mouths. I swished the sword in front of me to deter them, but they didn't seem to care.

Mr. Fletcher grabbed at me.

"Get back," I pleaded as I backed toward the porch. He lunged forward. I sliced his arm, but it didn't faze him. His wife hissed and swiped at me.

He grabbed at me again. This time he ignored the sword entirely and pushed the blade aside as he tried to grab me. I watched in horror as the shashka sliced his fingers off. They fell to the ground. Mrs. Fletcher, her feet bare and bloody, stepped on his dismembered fingers as she advanced. I ducked and dodged sideways. They pursued.

In that moment, I remembered what the man from the CDC had said: "brain activity." Victims were experiencing brain activity post-mortem. Was that what I was seeing?

They pursued me to the cabin steps. I quickly ascended to the top of the stairs. I looked down at those who had once been my neighbors.

"I'm sorry," I said, and having no other choice, I let the blade sing. Mrs. Fletcher was closest to me. Taking a couple of steps back, I made a running jump. I cleared the stairs, slicing off the top of her head as I passed. I turned as I landed. My cut had been a good one. Her erect body stumbled in a circle then fell. Mr. Fletcher let out a strange howl then lunged. With an under-hand to over-hand spin, the shashka twirled through the air; I sliced his head in half. He fell instantly. They both lay on the ground, jerking spastically. After a few moments, they fell still.

"Grandma!" I screamed. "Grandma!" I ran into the house, weapon in hand, but she was nowhere to be seen. My mind was half-bent on Ian, the other half worrying about my grandmother, as I headed to the barn and the guns. I grabbed the weapons, sliding the shashka back into the scabbard, then stuffed the Glock into a holster. I strapped the Colt around my shoulder and took the safety off the Magnum, holstering it as well. I grabbed three grenades and stuck them into my vest pockets. I headed out of the barn. As I turned the corner, I found myself face-to-face with what had once been my grandma. Her face was as pale as the moon; her eyes were an occluded mix of pearl white and veiny red. White froth dripped from her mouth.

I heard my grandmother's voice inside my head: *Kill me.*

I raised the Magnum. Just as my grandma lunged at me, I shot her between the eyes. She fell with a thud.

You see, my darling, kill-shot, I heard her say, and then I heard her no more.

Her body twisted once then fell into a peaceful slumber. I dropped to my knees beside her. Every fiber of my being wanted to pick her up and hold her. But then I remembered, the man from the CDC had said to avoid physical contact. I saw she had terrible bite marks on her hands.

"I love you," I whispered then rose, wiping tears from my eyes. I went to the tack room at the side of the barn and opened the door. There I found a Yamaha dirt bike, another of Grandma's recent purchases. I jumped on. It started with a kick. Careful to close and lock the gate behind me, I gunned the engine and peeled down Fox Hollow Road.

CHAPTER 6

FOX HOLLOW ROAD EMPTIED AT the base of Morrigon Hill. I made a sharp right toward the elementary school. I drove across the playground. At its other end, I found myself perched at the top of Kelly Street which looked down toward the community center. There were 50 or more of the sick outside. The crush of them had nearly broken down the door. The only other exit, the door to the medical center, was also surrounded.

Help them. I breathed deeply—in, out—I turned the bike and gunned it.

Moments later I dropped down onto Main Street. Around me, five or six of the diseased were moving toward the community center. I pulled out the Glock. "Brain activity," the man had said, "brain activity." I raised the gun and fired directly toward the brains of the sick, the . . . undead who lunged at me. The first three shots were a hit. For the last two, I missed again and again. Finally, I took down the woman. Just as he reached me, I managed to hit an over-sized man who I didn't recognize until the last second as Mr. Lewis, the hardware store owner. The realization made me feel sick to my stomach. He'd always been so kind, so funny, always had some stupid joke to share. And I'd shot him in the head. The sadness of everything threatened, but I blocked it out. I had to.

Distracted by the gun shots, some of the undead at the community center turned toward me.

"Please, please help me," I whispered, not sure who I was praying to. I pulled out one of the grenades and gunned the bike again. I dodged a few of the undead who tried to grab me, getting in as close as I could to the community center and the mass of undead crowded there, then slowed the bike for a split second. Pull the pin. Toss. Hit the gas.

The bike tire squealed as I hit the gas hard, turning toward the baseball field across from the community center. Seconds later the grenade exploded. The bodies of the undead flew everywhere. The roof of the community center porch collapsed, trapping the others.

Looking dazed, a group of about twenty or so undead began walking toward me. I sat still, letting them get a fix on me. Once they had clustered closely, I lobbed another grenade then tore out of there. It exploded with a bang that made my ears ring. Once I had gotten out of harm's reach, I stuffed a cartridge into the Colt. I hit the gas, speeding back onto Main Street. I was then thankful I had spent my youth and early adult life in fencing practice. With balance and dexterity that can only be acquired over time, I managed to drive with one hand and shoot with the other. I set off a spray of bullets into the remaining undead who wandered about aimlessly, confused by the sounds. I peeled the bike around and made a second pass, shooting any newcomers drawn in by the sound. At last, after several more shots, I didn't see any more of the undead moving. The place was still.

I pulled the bike into the parking lot and unsheathed the shashka. I stared at the building. I was only thirteen when my grandmother and I had come to the community center for a white elephant sale. Ethel, who was manning a benefit table, had asked my grandma if she could bring by a few donations. Grandma always had more knick-knacks than anyone could need. She'd come up with a box full of trinkets.

"What is a white elephant sale?" I remembered asking my grandma.

It was a windy spring day. It had been raining all morning, and light mist still dampened the air. Much to my teenage embarrassment, my grandma had donned her heavy yellow rain slicker and put on a plastic rain bonnet. She also wore three pink curlers in the front of her hair. No matter how long she wore those same three pink curlers, her bangs never curled. I huddled beside her under a partially broken black umbrella. Grandma had tried to give me a rain bonnet, but I couldn't take the humiliation.

"Ehh, it is like a yard sale. People sell their junk to each other," she replied as we walked toward the entrance.

"But why white elephant?"

"All a white elephant does is stand around, eat, and get looked at. What good does it do anyone?" she answered as she pushed open the door.

The room was full of treasure hunters, tables loaded down with tchotchkes, and town busybodies.

"Look around," my grandma directed as she headed toward Ethel's table.

I waved at Summer who sat beside her mother then went on a hunt for white elephants. Grandma was right. The place was full of junk. I passed table after table of glass vases, figurines, broken toys, old prom gowns, musty smelling luggage, and assorted dried flower arrangements. On one table, however, I found something unique. Mr. Beecher, a reptile of an old man, had recently closed up his antique shop. Displayed on his table, he had a number of leftover oddities. At once I was drawn to an old sword that lay amongst fishing gear, pocket knives, antique pens, and stainless steel lighters. I lifted the sword, but Mr. Beecher cautioned me.

"Careful, little Ruskie, it's sharp," he said.

I glared at him and pulled the sword from the scabbard. It was like love at first sight.

My grandmother came up beside me. "A shashka," she said. "Where did you find that?" she asked Mr. Beecher.

"Auction," he replied simply.

"What you want for it?" Grandma asked him.

Mr. Beecher turned serious. "Twenty."

"Ehh, no, no, no. I give you ten."

"Fifteen."

"I say I'll give you ten so I'll give you ten."

My grandmother never lost a negotiation. After a few more tries, Mr. Beecher finally consented, and Grandma started digging around in her sewing bag for the money. Ten dollars wasn't much, but for an old woman looking after a young girl, it was a fortune.

"Just look. Only someone like *that* would buy a sword for a little girl to play with," a woman sitting at the table next to Mr. Beecher whispered to her friend. The friend, a woman in a bright pink dress, laughed.

The three of us looked at the women. Giggling, they looked away. I recognized the woman who had gossiped about my grandma. She'd been to our house before. My grandmother looked long and hard at them both. She then turned, smiled at Mr. Beecher as she handed him the ten, and nodded to me that it was time to go. Her hand on my shoulder, she directed me toward the door.

"Thanks again," Ethel, who had not heard the rude comment, called with a wave.

My grandma smiled at Ethel but paused as we passed the gossips. "Next time you ask me if your husband is cheating, I won't lie to save your feelings. Talk to your friend. She knows more about it than I do," Grandma said. "You see, Layla, fools are not sown, they grow by themselves," she added then we left.

With my white elephant in hand, I smiled up at my grandma.

Now I moved toward the door of the same community center. A few of the fallen bodies twitched. A woman whose arms had been blow off by the grenade snapped at me. A snarling man who'd been blown in half pulled himself toward me. While I didn't recognize them, my heart felt heavy. This was my home. These were my townspeople lying under the roof: neighbors, old friends, classmates. It was abhorred to realize. I felt nauseous. Sighing deeply, I ended their lives. I then climbed onto the collapsed roof and carefully made my way to the door. Before I reached the entrance, two more undead appeared. Taking careful aim, I shot them.

When I got to the door, it was locked. I paused for a moment then knocked.

Jamie, Ian's older brother, opened the door. "Holy Christ, Layla! Is the Army out there or what?" he said looking over my shoulder. Seeing nothing, he looked me over, weapons hanging from every part of my body. "Jesus Christ," he said aghast and pulled me into a hug, dragging me inside. I suddenly felt overcome by everything that had just happened. I leaned heavily on Jamie. My body shook. I closed my eyes, but then realized everyone must have been looking at me. I took a deep breath and stepped back.

I recognized most of the faces in the room. Neighbors, teachers, the Ladies Auxiliary, the firemen, all faces I knew though some names I did not quite remember. Several people were injured. The school nurse, Mrs. Finch—how white her hair had become—was going from person to person trying to mend wounds.

My eyes scanned the room for Ian. He was kneeling on the floor beside Kristie who was bleeding profusely from a shoulder wound. She appeared to be in intense pain.

"Jamie, more will be drawn in by the noise. They are scattered everywhere, all over the town," I said, forcing myself to look away, to focus on something else.

Jamie nodded. "All right guys, we need to post a watch until we get ourselves together. Everyone with a gun muster up," Jamie called then turned to organize the group

Several of the men came up to me.

"Was that you out there, Layla?" Tom, one of the firefighters, asked. Tom had been in Jamie's class in school. Too shy to ask himself, he once sent his younger sister to ask me if I would go to a dance with him. Unfortunately for both Tom and me, I said no. I had a crush on a boy named Ian Campbell. As I looked up at Tom, however, I remembered that I'd always found his hazel eyes striking.

I nodded.

"Nice shooting," Gary, a squeaky little man with thick glasses, added. I remembered Gary somewhat. He used to come to Grandma's cabin to help her with her taxes. Gary shook my hand then followed Jamie's band of armed men outside.

"Thank you, oh, thank you, Layla," Ethel said, coming to kiss my cheeks. "Layla, where is Grandma Petrovich?"

I looked down and fought back my tears. Unable to speak, I just shook my head.

"Oh no," Ethel cried out, and turned, putting her head on Summer's shoulder.

"Sorry, Layla," Summer said and set her hand on my arm, "but thank you all the same. Good lord, where did you get those guns?" she asked absently as she guided her mother toward a seat.

I looked back into the room. Ian was calling for water. Kristie's cousin, April, was hovering over them. Kristie had gone into a seizure.

I followed the armed group outside. A couple of gunshots rang out as they took down a few of the approaching undead.

"Man, that's Mr. Corson. Here you go, asshole. Thanks for failing me in Chemistry," Jeff, Kristie's cousin, said with a laugh as he fired at the approaching man.

"Not cool, brother," Will, a high school aged relative of Summer and Ethel, chided him.

I leaned against the handicapped railing and looked at the bodies lying under the collapsed roof. Their arms and legs stuck out. I felt like I might be sick.

Jamie came and stood beside me. He eyed me over. "What are you doing here, Layla?"

I opened my mouth to explain when April came to the door. "Jamie, we can't talk any sense into Ian. Kristie's gone. We gotta put her down before she turns. He won't listen. Please, come help."

Jamie turned. I half followed but then heard Jeff.

"Someone ask Layla to do it. I'm sure she'd have no problem," he said.

Jamie stopped. "Can that shit right now, man. That's your cousin dying in there," he said, silencing Jeff. Then, casting an apologetic glance toward me, he went inside.

I turned back. Overhead, a hawk shrilled and flew out toward the lake. The creature had no the world was ending.

Then I heard grunting behind me. I turned to find a young child, perhaps seven or so years old, running toward me. Her mouth was dripping with bloody saliva. My hands shook. I pulled out the Magnum. I raised the gun and aimed. I couldn't pull the trigger. The little girl kept getting closer.

"Layla," I heard Tom call in warning behind me.

The girl got closer. I couldn't do it.

"Layla," Tom called again, panic filling his voice. A second later, a shot rang out. The girl fell with a thud.

I turned to look. Ian was standing on the collapsed roof, gun in his hand.

His eyes met mine. He cast me a knowing glance then went inside. Moments later, another shot—inside the building—was fired. I knew then that Kristie was dead.

CHAPTER 7

IT TOOK ABOUT TWO HOURS BEFORE the undead who had been drawn to the community center were dispatched. Inside, discussion then argument began about what to do next.

I stood by the door and listened. Tom, Mr. Jones who owned the local gas station, Jamie who had done two tours in Iraq as a medic, Pastor Frank from the Baptist Church, and Mrs. Finch seemed to be leading the discussion. Many of the others looked too scared or too shell-shocked to think let alone talk. Ian sat on the floor near Kristie's body, her face covered by someone's coat. He stared absently at his hands.

"What the hell are we gonna do now?" Jeff asked as he removed his hat and rubbed his sweaty forehead with his forearm.

"We need to gather all in one place," Mrs. Finch said, her finger pointing.

"No. We are safer in our own homes," Mr. Jones said.

"And what would I do in my house by myself? I don't have any guns. I have no way to protect myself. And lights are going to go off soon," Mrs. Finch retorted, her hands waving.

The more they talked, the more scared the rest of the group looked. Frenchie Davis' two children, apparently the only two kids yet to survive, clung to their mother.

"We should get out of town. We need to head toward a military base. We need to get somewhere safe, get help," Tom suggested looking at each of us in turn.

"The nearest base is more than 300 miles. We'll never make it," Jamie replied calmly.

"We don't even know what caused it," Mr. Jones said. "It could be anything. The food we eat. The water we drink. Something else in the environment. We don't even know if we can eat the supplies we have. All of us could still get sick. With the T.V. out, we've no idea what's happening."

"The 911 system went down yesterday, and now the phones are totally dead," Mrs. Finch added.

"Could be a bioweapon, a terrorist attack," Tom suggested.

Jamie shook his head. "Whatever it is, I heard it hit Canada too. It's spreading."

"It could simply be the wrath of God," Pastor Frank said solemnly.

Mrs. Finch frowned. "We need help. We need to all get together then head to a shelter, a base, something," she said, her fist pounding her hand to emphasize her words.

And on they went. Some voices started to rise. The louder they got, the more unsettled everyone else seemed. The children started to cry. Finally, at some point, no one could hear anyone else over the shouting.

I noticed then that there was an air horn canister on the shelf beside me. Frustrated, I picked it up and blew the horn. The *wooong* silenced the room.

"Right now we have no idea how many people are still alive in *this* town. We need to secure this place and get an accounting. First, we need to clear the dead bodies—we can bury them in the baseball field. Then we need to go around and see how many people are hiding in their houses. Once we have everyone accounted for, we can call a meeting and ensure people like Mrs. Finch are paired with others and can be kept safe—maybe we could use the elementary school as a base. This town is easy to defend. The lake has us protected on one side. The forest is on the other. There are only two roads and one bridge leading into this place. We need to get the town cleaned up then barricade the roads and put guards there."

"Well, Ms. Ancient-Warfare-Know-it-All," April began, "what about the bridge?"

Knowing how much April loved Kristie, I let it go. "We blow it up."

The room went silent.

"And how do we do that? I guess I could Google it, but the world just came to a fucking end," Jeff said.

"*Larry's Tree and Stump Removal* — he has dynamite."

Silence.

"She's right. We hunker down. We keep each other safe. Most of us here can hunt and fish. We can secure this place," Jamie said.

I smiled at Jamie.

With a half-smile, he tipped the brim of his hat toward me.

"Until help comes, right?" Ethel asked hopefully. Her obliviousness to the situation saddened me.

Jamie smiled softly at her. "Ethel . . . everyone . . . the reality is that help is not on the way. No reserves have been dispatched to Hamletville. I mean, they could barely evac New Orleans after Katrina. We're not exactly high up on a government list of priorities."

"We can be safe here, if we stick together," I offered.

Not everyone looked sure, but after some consideration, the survivors agreed to be divided into teams. Some were sent to patrol the streets. Some were sent to gather supplies and convene at the elementary school. Fred Johnson went to the town garage to get a backhoe to bury the dead. Jeff and a handful of others headed off to *Larry's Tree and Stump Removal*. After his comment outside, I secretly wished Jeff would blow himself up. We'd decided that two rings on the fire alarm meant assemble at the elementary school gymnasium, four rings if help had arrived, and six rings meant danger. Everyone was given medical gloves and strict advice to avoid touching dead bodies.

Ian and April moved Kristie's body from the community center to the baseball field. I watched Ian go. He did not look back. I went back to my dirt bike and got on. The body of the little girl still lay in the parking lot. I couldn't look at it.

I was about to kick start the engine when Jamie came up to me. "Where are you headed?"

"Home. I need to bury my grandma."

Jamie set his hand on my shoulder. His curly light brown hair, wet with sweat, stuck to his forehead. His blue eyes shined in the sunlight. He inhaled then exhaled heavily. "Sorry, Layla. Let me come help you."

Grateful, I smiled. "Thank you."

"You mind helping me with a little favor on the way?"

"Of course. What is it?"

"We have got to stop that bell ringing, or I am going to lose my mind," he said. The bell on the Catholic Church still sounded its melancholy gong.

"The world is ending, and you're worried about the bell?"

He smiled.

"All right. Hop on," I said, sliding forward.

"You won't even let me drive?"

"Are you kidding me?" I said and kicked the engine on.

"How humiliating," he muttered as he slid in behind me.

I parked the bike on the street in front of the church. The bell clanged loudly. Two of the undead who had been standing outside the church turned toward us. I raised my gun, but then recognized Mrs. Crane. She'd tutored me in math when I was in elementary school.

"Oh no," I said with a sigh. I lowered my gun.

Before she could get too close, Jamie shot her between the eyes.

The second sickly person, a man I didn't recognize, lumbered toward me. I downed him with a quick shot.

"You always were a good shot, Layla."

"Thanks to your dad. I didn't see—"

"He didn't make it. Neither him nor my mom."

"I'm so sorry. You and Ian—"

"Yeah, well, we all lost someone, right? I adored your grandma too. Come on. Let's get this over with."

When we walked up to the ornate doors, we both had a moment of realization. The place could be packed. Every Catholic in town could have taken shelter there.

I pulled the machine gun over my shoulder and stood at ready several feet from the door.

"Have any more grenades?"

"One. Let's hope we don't need it."

Jamie pulled out his handgun then yanked the doors opened.

We were half right; half the Catholics in town were inside. I pulled the trigger, peeling off a spray of bullets as the undead rushed out the door. I tried not to look at them too closely, knowing I would see familiar faces. The thought of it was too horrible. Jamie fired into the horde. Moments later, the space was clear, and a heap of bodies lay outside the door.

"Christ," Jamie said looking at the machine gun.

"I don't see how they miss with these things in the movies. At 1000 rounds a minute, who can miss?"

Jamie looked at the heap of bodies. His face twisted. "I know half the people lying there," he said. He closed his eyes and turned from the sight.

I had been trying not to think about it. "We don't have much choice," I said with more disconnect than I actually felt.

"After having to shoot my mom a dozen times before I figured out I needed a head shot, bumping off the meter man should be less jarring."

"Should? I don't know about that. You're no killer. But I'm sorry about your mom," I said, setting my hand on his shoulder. Jamie and his mom had always been very close, as close as Grandma and me. Grief tried to wash in. I slapped the door closed. After a lifetime of practice, I was good at doing that. I pulled out the shashka and looked up at Jamie.

"I'm ready," he said.

We went inside. An older woman I recognized from the farmer's market slowly crept out of the pew. She bit and snapped at us. I motioned Jamie to hold back, and I stabbed her through the eye. She dropped. We made our way toward the back of the church. Again, I caught sight of the broken Mary. It made me shudder.

We followed the winding halls to the back of the church. There found stairs leading up toward the bell tower. Carefully, we walked up the plank wood spiral staircase. The sweet scent of rough-cut lumber filled the air. When we reached the top, we discovered why the bell kept ringing. Father Meyers had hung himself with the bell rope. His body swayed back and forth.

"Guess he decided not to wait for the rapture," Jamie said, "which can occur any time now," he added with a raised voice as he looked toward the sky. He waited for a moment. "Nope, nothing," he said with a sardonic snort.

"Maybe he thought he was already in hell," I said, and reaching upward, I sliced the rope in half. Father Meyers's body fell on the wooden planks below. I stared down at the once-benevolent face now frozen in the grizzly visage of death. "I just saw him the other day. Grandma had me stop by."

"Why?"

"To ask for holy water."

"For what?"

"I don't know."

Jamie looked thoughtfully down at Father Meyers. "What do we do with him?"

I looked out the window. I noticed a newly opened grave in the graveyard. "There," I said, pointing.

"Well, it seems right to bury him, but how in the hell are we going to get him down?"

"Put on your gloves."

Jamie lifted Father from the left side. I lifted him from the right.

"Something about this seems wrong," Jamie muttered.

"1—2—3," I said, and with a heave, we dropped Father Meyers out the tower window. He fell with a thud on the ground.

"Well, he's already dead, and he had the courtesy not to get up and walk around. I'm sure he won't mind."

The church was clear when we exited. We dropped Father Meyers into the grave, covering him with a few inches of earth, then headed back toward the bike. On the way, however, we passed Mrs. Winchester's grave. I could not help but notice the dirt had collapsed in. I stopped to look.

"What is it?" Jamie asked.

"Mrs. Winchester was buried here—or is buried here. Her grave is disturbed."

Jamie stopped and looked with me. Moments later, the soil stirred.

"Christ," Jamie whispered. We watched in horror as fingers poked up through the soil. "How did she get out of her coffin?" Jamie wondered aloud as he started reloading his gun.

"Ethel said they did a green burial on her," I replied and took a step back. My eyes darted quickly around the graveyard. There were half a dozen or so fresh graves. Were all the residents stirring?

A second hand appeared. It grabbed at the grass, pulling the body upward. We stood frozen with shock as Mrs. Winchester slowly dragged herself out of the earth. It was too horrible. Her hair was covered in soil, and her flesh was drooping. The rancid smell of decay wafted from her, turning my stomach. When her head was finally clear of the ground, Jamie raised his gun and fired; he hit her between her rheumy eyes.

With a gurgling cry, Mrs. Winchester's body, half out of the earth, went still.

"Oh my god," I whispered. Tears flooded my eyes.

Jamie grabbed my hand. "Let's go."

I took one last look at a woman who had once been so kind to me, and then we walked away.

We set off back toward Fox Hollow Road. When we got back to the cabin, the Fletchers' bodies were still lying beside the steps, and Grandma lay in front of the barn where I had left her.

"I'm so sorry," Jamie said at the sight.

I nodded, and we got to work. Behind the barn, we dug one wide grave for the Fletchers and a second grave for my grandmother. Wearing gloves, we lowered the bodies in. We covered the Fletchers first. Gross as it was, I retrieved Mr. Fletcher's fingers too. Then we lowered Grandma into her grave. Once her eyes had been closed, my grandmother actually looked very peaceful. I wanted to kiss her one last time, to feel the soft skin on her cheek, but I dared not come too close to her flesh. I started to cry.

Jamie wrapped his arms around me. I turned toward him. He enveloped me in his thick chest, holding me tightly against him.

"I'm sorry," was all he could say. "I'm so sorry."

Turning, I inhaled deeply. Composing myself, I grabbed the shovel and began to cover my grandmother with earth. Grief wracked me.

Now, now, it's only a husk, I heard my grandmother say.

I stopped and looked around.

"Layla?" Jamie asked.

"Did you hear that?"

"Hear what?"

I looked down at my grandmother. She lay still in the repose of death.

"Nothing," I said and began again.

Not long after, we finished.

"Why don't you come in? Drink something? Wash up?" I asked Jamie.

"I should get back to Ian," he said.

I nodded. I opened the back of my SUV and took out the weapons bundle. I then handed the keys to Jamie. "Take my SUV."

"You sure?"

"Well, it saved me once already today. No doubt it will keep you safe too. Thank you, Jamie, for everything. You've always been like the brother I never had," I said and leaned in to hug him.

A strange look crossed his face, but he covered it quickly, returning my embrace.

"I'll be back tomorrow morning. You can help me with the canvassing," he said as he slid into the driver's seat and turned on the engine. "Nice," he added with a smile as he ran his hand over the dash.

I grinned. I went to the gate and pulled it open for him. "Stay safe," I called.

He waved. "You too. Lock that gate."

I nodded and shut the gate with a clang, locking it as he drove out of sight.

Moments later there was complete silence. In the distance I could hear the stream gurgling and the sweet sound of songbirds. The wind blew, picking up the earthy autumn air. I turned to go back into the house but spotted my grandma's herb bag lying on the ground near the gate. I picked it up and looked inside. She had picked a large bouquet of wildflowers. Had she died for this, died for a handful of flowers? I walked back to her grave and laid the flowers thereon. Then, all at once, it hit me. She had not died because she'd gone to pick flowers. She already knew how she would die. She'd already seen the grave. She'd already seen the flowers. She'd just saved me the trouble of picking them for her. All this time, she knew she was not going to make it. Everything she'd done, she'd done to save me—not her and me—just me.

Tears flooded my eyes. I allowed myself a moment of grief and then pulling myself together the best I could, I went inside. After all, "it's only a husk." She had said it. And I had heard it. I had not imagined it. I had heard my grandmother's voice.

CHAPTER 8

FOR THE TIME BEING, there was still hot water and electricity. I took a long shower. Wrapping myself in a thick white robe, I poured myself a large glass of vodka. The sun had set. I flipped on the small living room lamp and sat down on the floor. My cell had died—no signal—but the old mantel clock showed it was nearly 11:00pm. The autumn air had a hint of chill in it. I lit a small fire.

I knew I should eat, but I couldn't get myself to budge. I sat, staring at the fireplace. I tried to process everything, but I felt completely overwhelmed. How had this happened? What were we going to do? My grandma was gone.

The radio in Grandma's room still reported contamination and quarantine. After a while, I realized it was the same news report I'd heard that very morning; it was a looped recording. I tried the T.V. but there was only static.

It must have been sometime after midnight, and two glasses of vodka later, when I saw headlights shine through the small cracks between

65

the boards on the picture window. I went outside to see a truck sitting on the other side of the gate.

I grabbed a gun. "Who's there?" I called, the headlights blinding me.

At first there was silence. The driver cut the lights and engine. "It's Ian."

My heart leapt to my throat. I grabbed the flashlight, slid on a pair of slippers, and went to the gate.

"It's late," I said.

His face looked haggard in the glow of the flashlight.

"I know. I'm sorry. I just . . . can I come in?"

I unbolted the gate. I propped it a little, letting him in, then locked it again. Wordlessly, we went into the house. Once inside, I motioned him to sit in the living room while I went to the kitchen to pour him a drink.

"God, Layla, when did you get the house all boarded up?"

"Grandma," I replied.

"Jamie told me about her. I'm really sorry."

I handed him a drink and sat down on the couch beside him. He looked handsome but tired. His straw-colored hair fell over his blue eyes. He had dirt smudged on his chin and arms. His tribal tattoo showed from under his torn and stained white t-shirt. I wondered if anyone else knew the tattoo's meaning.

"I'm a mess," he said.

"That's the last thing to worry about."

"But you smell so clean, so nice," he whispered.

"Well, I figured I should take a hot shower while I still had a chance."

He smiled then there was awkward silence. Every fiber in my being wanted to pull him into an embrace, to smell him, to feel his chest pressed against my body, but I reminded myself his wife had died only hours before.

"Why are you here?" I asked.

He shook his head. "Layla . . . I . . . When it all started to go down, I tried to keep my family safe, but I kept thinking, 'Where is Layla? Is Layla all right?' I was praying to God you were not still in D. C. Did you see? They rained missiles down on that place. Blew it up. It was one of the last things I saw on cable. I thought I saw your car the other day so I hoped. But when Jamie opened the door today, and I saw you standing there, I couldn't believe it. At that moment Kristie was dying, but you were alive. I felt happy. I am so ashamed. I felt so happy."

"I seriously hope you didn't come here just to confess," I said. Part of me was elated, but the other half of me was disgusted.

"No. I just wanted to see you. I wanted to tell you how I felt. I'm so happy you're fine. You're alive. And you're here. I just, Layla, you know I never stopped loving you," he said then pulled me toward him. Before I knew it, we had fallen into a deep kiss.

How much I had missed him. Every muscle in my body melted. My mind, swimming in a vodka haze, let go of guilt. I relaxed into his embrace. My hands greedily roved over his shoulders, neck, and under his shirt to touch his skin.

Untying my belt, he pushed the robe open. I was naked underneath. He kissed my neck and shoulders, his hands gently stroking my breasts. I shimmied out of the robe and pulled his shirt over his head. I pulled him against me, his bare skin against mine. We lay back on the couch. I could feel him, hard, inside his jeans. I took his hand to guide it between my legs, but when my fingers interlaced with his, I felt his wedding ring. Shame washed over me. I opened my eyes. I pulled myself upright and slid my robe back on.

"Layla?"

I stood up, picked his shirt up, and threw it at him.

"Get out," I said.

"Layla? What happened?"

"You can't solve every complex feeling you have by fucking someone. Get out. Go home and mourn your wife like a real man would," I said and opened the door.

Shame faced, he pulled his shirt on and went outside. He stopped on the porch. "I'm sorry. I didn't come here for that. I just came to say I am so glad you're alive," he said and walked away.

I slammed the door behind him. Outside, the metal gate opened and shut. A moment later the truck started, and the headlights disappeared back down the road. I slid down the door to the floor and put my head on my knees. Then there was a strange buzzing sound, like the sound you hear during a bad storm, followed by a pop. The lights and all the appliances went out.

"Dammit," I whispered.

The fire had burned down to a bank of embers. I felt around the kitchen table for the candles. Grandma had left a box of them sitting there. Striking a match, I lit a candle and turned toward the living room.

I nearly screamed. My grandmother was sitting in her favorite chair in front of the fireplace doing crochet. Like the Native American chief, I saw my grandmother and saw through her all at once. *Don't forget to lock the gate*, she said without looking up.

I turned toward the door, considering her words, then turned back. When I did, she was gone, but her sewing was sitting on the chair, and I couldn't remember if it had been there all along or not.

Taking the flashlight and my shashka, I went outside. I could hear a strange *clang, clang, clang* noise as I walked toward the gate. At the gate was a young woman whose face was so badly torn apart I couldn't recognize her. Her entire nose had been torn off, revealing fleshy pulp inside. She must have followed Ian's truck up the road. She was pushing at the gate, biting and snapping when she saw me.

I kept my flashlight on her and got close. We stood across from one another locked in a stare. I wondered about "brain activity." Clearly, the undead hungered, but did they think? In that same moment, I also realized she had a bright red ribbon in her hair.

I felt confused and frustrated. "Stop," I commanded and for a moment she was still. But then she snapped and snarled again.

I sighed. I lifted the sword and thrust it through her skull. She fell like a bag of bones. I locked the gate and headed inside, barring the door behind me. This time I went directly to bed. While my grandmother lived on in the spirit, the world was now filled with the undead, and I'd had enough fighting the undead for one day.

CHAPTER 9

I WAS SITTING ON THE FRONT porch drinking fire-brewed coffee when Jamie pulled up in my SUV. I swished the truly awful coffee around in my mouth. It was bitter and laced with grounds. I dumped the remaining liquid over the side of the porch and went to let Jamie in.

"Power out here too?" he asked.

I nodded. "I'd offer you some coffee, I made it over the fireplace, but I think you'd never forgive me. Looks like Grandma forgot to stock up on instant."

"Well, maybe she wanted you learn how to cook."

"Nothing like the apocalypse to force us to learn new skills."

We both laughed.

"You ready?"

I was already dressed, my weapons reloaded. I'd added throwing daggers to my belt and had slid the poyasni into my boots. I patted the shashka. "You bet."

Closing up everything behind us, we headed down Fox Hollow Road.

"So what's the plan?" Jamie asked.

"I have an idea, but we need the police cruiser. Do you think that will be a problem?"

Jamie shook his head. "The guys have already been in the Sheriff's Office to clear out the guns. The car is still sitting there."

"Ok, first we get the car."

We drove across town to the Sheriff's Office. It was a small building that sat close to the river. The cruiser was parked outside. We exited the SUV carefully, keeping an eye out for the undead. The door to the office was open. When we reached the doorway we could hear grunting coming from inside.

"I thought this place was clear," I whispered.

"It was."

We couldn't see anyone when we first entered. Ducking low, we crept around the front desk. There was an old man in the break room. He was rocking back and forth; his clothes were ragged, and one arm was clearly dislocated.

Jamie stood, raising his gun, but I stopped him. I patted my throwing daggers. Careful to get into position, I unsheathed one dagger and, sending it over hand, launched it through the air. It hit him squarely in the back of the head. He fell with a thump.

"I think you're on steroids," Jamie said with a grin.

I shook my head. "No, I just practice and work out a lot."

"So I see," Jamie replied, playfully eyeing me over.

I grinned. Jamie always loved to tease me. "I'll get the knife. Grab the keys?"

He nodded and headed toward the desk.

I headed toward the break room to retrieve my knife. The body of the old man lay on the floor. When I turned the corner, however, I got jumped. An enormous undead man had been standing in a blind spot. We'd missed him. When I walked in, he attacked. Seconds later he slammed me to the floor. I hit the ground hard. "James!" I screamed.

The massive undead man lay sideways on top of me. He snapped at me, his mouth a mess of mangled flesh and bloody saliva. I struggled to keep him from making contact with my skin. I tried to push him off, but he was too heavy.

Jamie was there the next second and kicked the man off of me. The undead man fell to the floor and with one shot, Jamie took him out.

"Oh my god, oh my god," I whispered, frantically pulling off my shirt and gloves. Had his flesh touched mine?

"Pants too," Jamie said in a rush and helped me unbuckle my belt. Seconds later I stood in the middle of the Sheriff's office, completely naked save my bra and underwear, my entire body shaking.

"Did it touch your skin? Did it get any saliva on you?"

I shook my head. "No, no, I don't think so.

Jamie grabbed me by the arm and pulled me to the sink where we washed down my arms and legs with the icy cold water. I scrubbed my arms while Jamie scrubbed my legs and waist. Something made my stomach lurch with an emotion far different than fear as I felt Jamie's wet hands sliding gently around my body. My eyes fluttered closed.

"No signs of contamination. Skin looks good," Jamie said, eyeing me over. "Oh my god, Layla."

I stood shaking. Too many emotions overwhelmed me.

"I'll go to the back and get you something to put on," he said.

Shivering, I waited. We needed to be more careful. My stomach rolled. I didn't want to think about it, any of it. If I let the terror in, it would be too much. I was okay. We were both okay.

Minutes later Jamie returned with a standard issue police uniform, fingerless leather gloves, and a brown leather jacket. I pulled the clothes on and, still shaking, went back out front.

"Christ, my heart is still beating in my throat," Jamie whispered.

"I'm okay," I said, feeling less certain than I sounded.

"You sure?" Jamie asked, peering closely at me.

I shrugged. What choice did I have? "Let's go."

Jamie grabbed the keys, and we headed toward the car.

"Go to the end of Main Street, and we'll start from there," I said, trying to refocus. "We'll need to use the PA speaker system, but we're bound to attract company."

Jamie set two guns on the seat beside him. "We're good."

He drove the police cruiser toward the end of town the made the turn back. He slowed the car. I grabbed the CB and flipped the speaker system on.

"Test. Hamletville citizens, test," I said into the speaker as Jamie adjusted the volume. "Are you alive inside? Hang a white cloth out a window if you are alive. Hang a red cloth if you are injured. Hang black if there are undead inside with you," I projected.

"Assuming their clothes aren't in the wash," Jamie said.

Finally relaxing, I punched him playfully on the shoulder.

And so we began to make our passes, street by street, repeating the message. It was not long until the aimless undead were drawn by the sound of my voice. When we hit Briar Street we found ourselves facing a small horde of a dozen undead. At the front I recognized Paul Lacombe, the town's mailman. My grandma used to leave a tin of cookies in the mailbox for him every year at Christmas time. With regret, we jumped out of the police car and took Paul and the others out. We cruised up and down the street, announcing all morning. By noon or so, we had hit every street. We then stopped by the community center and rang the fire alarm twice. After, we headed toward the elementary school.

We found a dozen people already assembled inside the gym. Tom and Jeff were standing guard at the door. Those inside had been busy stocking the place with supplies.

"Oh, thank goodness," Mrs. Finch said when she saw us. "We have a minor problem," she added and pulled us to the side. "Jamie, I didn't want to tell Tom, but his little niece, Karie, has gone bad. We locked her in Mrs. White's classroom. I just didn't know how Tom would take it. He's lost everyone else. I think he was holding out hope for her. Can you please take care of her?" Mrs. Finch told us.

I looked at Jamie and shook my head. "No, he should know."

Jamie looked back and forth from Mrs. Finch to myself and then to Tom. "It may break him. That guy is mush on the inside."

"Should we let him have false hope while one of us executes his niece?"

"Oh Jamie, just do it," Mrs. Finch said, ignoring me.

I shook my head. "I'll talk to him."

"Layla," Mrs. Finch grumbled.

"He should decide, not us," I replied and went to Tom.

Mrs. Finch was clearly angry but said nothing. She went back to work, slamming boxes from one table onto another. I approached Tom carefully.

"Hey Tom, can you come with me? Jamie will take your post for a minute," I said, taking hold of Tom's arm.

"Well, good morning, Layla," Jeff said with a raunchy smile. "Hey, wasn't that Ian's truck I saw going up Fox Hollow Road last night?"

I glared at him.

Jamie raised a questioning eyebrow but said nothing.

I pulled Tom away.

"What is it?" Tom asked as we passed through the gym and into the classroom hallway.

"You heard my grandma got sick?" I asked him.

"Yeah, someone mentioned it. Sorry to hear it."

"I had to put her down myself. I almost couldn't do it. But you know my grandma, always on about the spirits. I think I heard her tell me to kill her. Can you believe that? I heard her in my head. She said 'kill me.' So I did. It was the worst moment of my life." There was only minor risk in telling him. Before his wedding, Tom had come to see Grandma. Shortly thereafter he called off the wedding. I often wondered what Grandma had seen that so convinced him.

"I don't know what to say," Tom said. He gazed down at me with a confused look on his face.

We were standing outside Mrs. White's classroom door.

"They tell me your niece, Karie, is inside," I said, motioning to the door. "I can handle it if you want, but I thought it should be your decision."

Tom inhaled sharply, his hand covering his mouth.

Drawn by the noise, Karie appeared on the other side of the door. Her face looked almost like a China doll: her pale white skin was surrounded by a halo of black hair. But there was no mistaking those undead eyes and the frothy drool coming from her mouth.

Tom stared at her, wiping the tears from his eyes. He took a deep breath and then backed up to the wall. He loaded his gun and aimed toward the door.

I took a few steps away to avoid the spray of glass. I turned my back.

"I'm sorry, baby," I heard him whisper.

Boom. The sound of the shot-gun echoed in the hallway and made my ears ring. I heard the little body hit the floor with a thud.

Tom slid down the wall and put his head on his knees. He wept. "I was there when she was born. They put that newborn baby in my hands. I was the one who showed her to my sister," he moaned through tears.

I sat beside him, my arm around his back, my head leaning on his shoulder. What could I say? Despair was all around us. It was too much to bear if you let it in. The grief was palpable. Tears welled up in my eyes. I could not imagine shooting a child, alive or dead. In a heartbeat, we had all become killers, slaughtering those we loved the most. It was unnatural. My grandmother's ashen face appeared before my eyes again. It was too horrible. I forced myself to take a deep breath and push the image away. We sat there for a long time listening to the sound of occasional gunfire outside the school. After a while, Jamie appeared.

"Everyone is ready," he said.

I nodded and rose.

Standing up, Tom wiped his eyes. "Thank you," he said, hugging me, and then he headed back to the gym. Jamie and I followed him.

"You were right," Jamie whispered as he cast a glance toward Tom. Before we entered, Jamie stopped. He took my hand and looked carefully at me. "Layla, was Ian at your place last night?"

I gave Jamie's hand a squeeze. It was not what Jamie was thinking, but I was not really sure what had happened between Ian and me. I also wasn't sure why the look on Jamie's face made me feel so embarrassed. Jamie and I had always been friends—he was Ian's brother after all—but suddenly I felt worried about what he thought of me. In the end, I said nothing but walked hand-in-hand with Jamie into the gym.

When we entered, Ian spotted us. A strange look of shame and jealousy washed over his face. All the eyes in the gym turned toward me.

Jamie smiled down at me. "Go ahead," he said, urging me toward the front of the crowd.

"Me? You're the one with all the military experience."

"Yeah, but I didn't blow up the community center yesterday nor am I a historian who knows everything about warfare."

"Ancient warfare."

"Well, clearly, the medieval period is back in style."

"Me?"

"It has to be you."

I balked for a moment then, taking a deep breath, went to the front. I jumped up on the stage. I then remembered my third grade Christmas play.

We'd enacted a living Christmas tree. I played the tinsel. Grandma had sewn me a shiny gold and silver costume. Ian had played a snowflake.

"Hello, everyone. You all probably heard the announcements we made this morning. Hopefully our neighbors have hung their houses with white, red, or black flags. We need to get the living, those with the white flags, accounted for and brought up to speed on the plan to keep the town safe. Jamie and Mrs. Finch should go with teams to attend to the houses with red flags. Please be careful. We have no idea if those injuries are a broken arm or the bite from an undead. Black flags? Well, we need an armed team to handle those houses. If there is no flag, that likely means the house is either empty or there are undead inside. Look for survivors. Kill the undead. We'll divide into groups. Any questions?"

"Sounds good, Layla," Pastor Frank said, "but the other problem is that the power is out now. I don't have a fireplace. What should I do?"

I spotted a rolling whiteboard and pulled it onto the stage. I grabbed a marker and drew a grid on the board. "If you're armed, put your name here. If you have a fireplace, a way to heat your home, put your name here. If you have need, put your name and your need here. We need to open our homes and our hearts if we want to make it through the winter."

"Layla," a voice called from the back.

I scanned around until I spotted an older gentleman in a marigold colored CAT baseball cap. A lit cigarette hung from his mouth. It was Larry. Now we had someone to handle dynamite. I was relieved.

"The boys found me yesterday and told me the plan to blow up the bridge. I can have it rigged by tomorrow. I just need a careful hand or two to help," he said.

"Volunteers?" I called.

Mr. Jones and another young man I did not know raised their hands.

"There you go, Larry. Thanks guys."

"Layla, we need more weapons. We've cleared out the Lewis' shop and the Sheriff's Office, but it's still not enough. And we really need more ammo," Will said.

"What about the VFW? They got anything there?" I asked.

Will shook his head. "Just antiques."

"They've got a working cannon. We could use that," Jeff said.

"Dude, what are you gonna do with a cannon? We're not fighting the British armada," Will replied.

Jeff gave Will the finger.

"What about Mara Hunting Club?" Summer asked. "Mom and I cater out there. I think they leave guns locked up there all year round."

"There we go. Tomorrow morning we need to get to work on barricades and some of us can head out to Mara. Those who can help should meet back here just after dawn."

Everyone nodded.

"Let's get everyone into groups for the town sweep," Jamie called out. "Keep track of who or what you find and at what addresses," he added, then began putting people into teams.

As Jamie moved through the crowd, I counted. Forty-seven. That was all that was left. Granted, it was not a large town and there were many out-lying farms, but out of nearly 600 or so, forty-seven was not much. I jumped off the stage.

I noticed then that Frenchie was there with her children. It was hard to miss her fiery red hair which fell, disheveled, to her waist. She was filling tote bags with canned goods.

"Hey Frenchie," I called as I came over to her. I barely remembered her from high school. She'd always been the quiet type. She'd gone off to college but came home a year later pregnant—no dad in the picture. Her older child, who also had red hair, looked to be about six, the younger about four. She seemed really alone. Last I knew she was living in a trailer near Griswold Cemetery.

"Hey, Layla. Thanks for everything you're doing," she said, trying to sound confident when her voice and every line on her face told me otherwise. I eyed her over. She already looked gaunt. I could not imagine what she must have endured to keep her children safe. "These are my girls, Kira and Susan," she introduced.

I knelt down to look at them. "Who is Kira and who is Susan?" I asked.

"I'm Kira," the older child with red hair said. "She is Susan."

"You're pretty," Susan, the younger girl with pixie-like features, told me.

I smiled at them. "Not as pretty as the two of you," I said, tapping them each on the nose. I rose. "Frenchie, I was thinking, why don't you and the girls stay with me? The place is locked down. I'm remote so there is less potential for traffic. And I'm well stocked. You'll be safe there."

The girls looked up at her with eager anticipation.

"You sure?" she asked.

"Of course. We'll get you moved in today."

She set down her tote bags and wrapped her arms around me. Her body was shaking. "Thank god. My girls . . ." she whispered in my ear.

"It's okay. I'll keep them safe," I whispered in reply. I hoped it was a promise I could keep.

CHAPTER 10

OUTSIDE THE GYMNASIUM FIVE ARMED men stood smoking cigarettes, shot-guns hanging over their shoulders. I recognized them but didn't know their names. "We're on watch here," one explained, and I nodded affirmatively.

I knew that my stunt at the community center had earned me respect, but I was not quite comfortable with the idea of being the leader of Hamletville. Not sure what to do with myself, I decided to head out to join one of the sweep teams. I found a team outside the Franklin house. By chance, Ian was there. Ian, Jensen, Dusty, and Gary were staring up at the black shirt hanging from an upstairs window of the run-down Victorian mansion.

Shamefaced, Ian looked away from me.

"Hey Layla," Jensen said as I joined them. "We're just thinking of a plan of attack."

"If someone goes around back and makes a lot of noise, whatever is inside will be drawn that direction. The rest of us can go in from the front and get the jump on them," Ian suggested.

"Is the door locked?" I asked.

"Not sure," Dusty answered.

"I'll go around back. I can haul ass if needed," Gary said then left. We waited. A few moments later we heard Gary in the back banging garbage can lids. "Come and get it! Fresh meat on blue light special in the backyard," he called.

I had to laugh. Gary was seemingly one of the least funny men I'd ever met. I guess he was full of surprises too.

The others laughed as well.

"Got some action in the window back here," Gary yelled after a minute.

Dusty, Jensen, Ian, and I stepped cautiously onto the porch. Dusty tried the door. "Locked," he whispered.

Ian pulled his shotgun to blast the lock, but I stopped him. I lifted the ladybug print *Welcome* mat. The key was underneath.

"And there's why we put you in charge," Dusty said with laugh.

I grinned and handed Ian the key.

In the back, Gary was still slamming garage can lids, and I started to worry about anyone else who might be lurking about in earshot.

We went in. The old Victorian had seen better days. Plaster crumbled off the filigree trim around the ceiling. The rose pattern wallpaper looked faded. It looked like there had been a tussle in the living room. We could hear groaning and the sound of a body slamming against the door in the back.

"There might be more than one," I whispered, my memory of the incident in the Sheriff's Office still fresh.

Jensen nodded and waved us toward the left side of the house into the dining room. I bent one ear upstairs but heard nothing. The dining room was beautifully bedecked with dark navy brocade wallpaper. A slightly tarnished tea service sat on a cherry server. The formal dining room had a small serving window that looked into the kitchen. In the back, Mrs. Franklin clawed at the back door.

"Got her," Jensen whispered then took aim.

"Watch out for Gary," Ian cautioned.

I turned away, unsheathing my sword, keeping one eye on the dining room entryway.

Bam. The hunting rifle discharged with a loud boom that made the chandelier rattle.

A moment later I heard a flurry of feet from the other side of the house. Surprisingly fast for being undead, a young woman, Jenna, caretaker for many of the town's elderly, emerged from a side room and lunged at me.

"Layla!" Ian called out.

Jumping onto a dining room chair, then onto the table, I spun, the sword slicing through the air. I severed Jenna's skull in half. Her momentum caused her body to fling forward. It hit the table and buckled. The severed head spilled a mush of brains and blood onto the table.

"Gross," Jensen said.

"Dammit, she was fast," Dusty cursed.

We all paused and waited, listening. My heart was pounding.

"Let's check upstairs," Ian whispered.

When we got back to the foyer, Gary joined us.

"Better keep guard," I told him. "You might have gotten someone else's attention."

"I'm on it," he said and took a post on the porch.

When we got upstairs, Ian called out. "Anyone alive up here?"

We waited.

A moment later we heard slow footsteps. Everyone raised a weapon. One of the bedroom doors opened, and an elderly man stood clutching the doorframe. It was Mr. Franklin. Clearly, he was not in good health, and he looked frightened out of his mind.

"My wife," he whispered, rasping.

"I'm sorry, Mr. Franklin, she's dead," Dusty told him.

He nodded sadly and took a puff on his inhaler.

"Come sit down," I said, sheathing my sword. I guided the old man back into the room and to a chair. The room smelled like body odor, urine, and moldy food. He must have been locked in there for several days.

"Mr. Franklin, we need to move you. You're not safe all alone in the house. Let us take you to stay with someone," Dusty encouraged.

"Mrs. Finch is going to move in with Fred Johnson. That might be a good place for him," Ian suggested.

"My medicines," the old man said, motioning toward the table.

My stomach hurt. There was no way this man would survive. Just like Frenchie's children, he was so vulnerable. The enormity of keeping such people safe overwhelmed me.

"I got them," I said and rose. I unzipped a pillowcase and put all the medicines inside.

Dusty and Jensen helped Mr. Franklin downstairs. Outside, Gary shot twice at an approaching undead man. I could only see the shadow of their figures through the beveled glass windows.

Mr. Franklin stopped at the bottom of the steps. "What's happening?" he asked.

"It's the end of days," Dusty replied. "Come on, Mr. Franklin. The good Lord hasn't called you just yet."

The old man muttered in reply.

When I reached the bottom of the stairs, I noticed Mr. and Mrs. Franklin's wedding portrait hanging on the wall. They looked so young and happy.

Ian came up behind me. He stopped and looked at the photo as well. "I want to talk about last night," he whispered, but I raised my hand to cut him short.

"Not now," I said and went outside. Who would have thought that the end of the world would bring me the one thing I wanted most. I did still want him, didn't I?

CHAPTER 11

THE SUN HAD JUST PEEKED over the mountains when we collected in the elementary school parking lot the following morning. The sunrise was a mix of pink and orange. The air was cool. Mist was rising off the lake and river. Half the streets were shrouded in fog. It was amazingly quiet: no cars, no hum of electricity, no nothing, just birds and the sound of the wind.

About two dozen people had assembled.

I rubbed my gloved hands together. "We need to get some barricades in place at both ends of Main Street. Is Fred here?" I asked, looking around.

"Here, Layla," he called.

"You're our man, Fred. What have we got? What can we roll in?"

"I need about ten bodies to help. We can drive in the old school buses and fill the gaps with scrap, dumpsters, barrels and the like," he replied.

"I think I saw that in a movie once," Jeff muttered.

"The Williams folks just had a ton of chain link fencing delivered to expand their kennels. It's still rolled up on their property. We could try to fence the barricade as well," Jensen offered.

"Sounds good."

"Layla, this is Kiki Jones. She's Lil's and Wilson's daughter—they didn't make it. She had an idea," Tom said.

Kiki's eyes were red and swollen from crying. Dark rings made half-moons under her brown eyes. "Well," Kiki started, "I did a project at college with short wave radios. I might be able to get a radio up and running. Maybe we can see if there are other survivors out there. But I need to see if there is some equipment in the school."

"Great idea," I said, smiling encouragingly at her, "take whatever you need." She reminded me of my fencing students. I choked down the wave of despair that bubbled up as I realized they were probably all dead.

"I can give a hand with that," Gary told Tom and Kiki. "I used to play around with the CB. I have some stuff that might help."

"All right then. Let's split up. This group can go with Fred," I said, portioning off the crowd. "The rest of you will keep patrol. We need to set up a schedule, get on rotating shifts. Jensen, can you put that together and let people know when they are on patrol?"

He nodded affirmatively.

Summer waved at me. "I'll come with you to Mara Hunting Club. They have bulk food stored up there, and I have a key," she said, dangling a key chain in front of her.

"Great, let's go," I called and everyone moved out.

Jamie, Summer, and I packed into my SUV. Ian, Will, and Dusty headed out in Ian's truck. We crossed town and turned up Morrigon Hill. I sat in the back while Jamie drove. Summer tried the radio stations. There was nothing but static.

"How is it that everything just stops?" Summer asked. "It all just stopped." She snapped off the radio.

"I haven't seen an airplane in days. Sky is completely empty," I added as I looked out the window. We passed a dense pine forest, the green needles making a thick canopy, the ground covered in pink needles.

"Makes you wonder, right? How many man-made things out there are dependent on electricity, oil, fuel? With no one around to push a button, what prevents missiles from going off or dams from collapsing?" Jamie questioned.

"I guess we're screwed either way," I said, popping a cartridge into my gun. I rolled down the window. "Slow up," I called to Jamie.

An undead man plodded out of the woods and into the ditch that led downhill toward town. As we rolled up on him, he stopped and looked at the SUV. I leaned out the window and took a shot. His neck snapped back as the bullet hit him between the eyes, and he fell into the ditch.

"Christ, that water runs downhill and into the stream," Jamie said, putting the SUV into park.

I grabbed some medical gloves and jumped out, handing a pair to Jamie. We pulled the gloves on and went over to the body.

"Recognize him?" I asked as we stood over the body.

Jamie shook his head.

We lifted the heavy man, carried him to the bank, and dropped him into the forest. We climbed back into the SUV.

Summer was staring out the window at the dead body.

"We need to tell people to boil their water," Jamie said as he put the SUV back in gear.

Summer rolled the window back up. "Blessed are the meek for they shall inherit the earth," she recited absently, "the beatitudes, Matthew 5.5. Yeah, right."

Neither I nor Jamie knew what to say. We rode in silence the rest of the way to Mara Hunting Club.

When we got there, Ian's truck was parked at the very end of the long driveway. The club sat in the middle of a large field. The shooting range was set down in a pit with an earthen retaining wall. From the end of the driveway you could see the roof above the shooting stand. The club itself was a large log cabin with arching windows that looked out onto the field.

What caught us all off guard was the fact that there were cars in the parking lot. There was not another town within an hour's driving distance. Who was there?

"Was there an event or something?" I asked Summer.

She looked surprised. "Not that I know of."

We got out of the SUV and joined Ian's group. I'd brought my binoculars with me. I crawled into the back of Ian's truck and leaned on the roof. I focused the binoculars to get a better look.

"See anything?" Ian asked.

I scanned the place. There was no movement anywhere. Nothing moved at the shooting range nor could I see anything through the windows. "No movement in the building." I looked toward the parking lot. "Nothing is moving, but there are two vans and six cars in that parking lot." I jumped out of the back of the truck and stared at the building. My hands were shaking. Something felt off. Something felt wrong.

"Okay, let's go," Ian said.

Jamie read the expression on my face. "What is it? What's wrong?"

"I don't know. Something."

Ian started pulling guns out of the back of his truck. "It's clear. Let's move."

"Naa Ian, not like that," Jamie said, taking one look at me then back at the building. Jamie turned and gave Will a knowing look.

Will nodded and took off in a sprint across the grassy field, keeping as low as possible in the tall weeds.

I lifted the binoculars and watched him go.

"Do you always have to be right, man?" I heard Ian grumble at Jamie.

"Just being cautious," Jamie answered.

Will moved quickly, and soon he was at the building. "He's clear so far," I said. I watched as Will looked into the windows of the club. He flashed me an *okay* sign then dodged around the back of the building out of sight. I held my breath. We waited.

Moments later, Will came running from behind the building. He was dashing quickly through the grass. "They're coming," he yelled. "They're coming," he screamed again as he ran toward us.

Seconds later, cresting over the shooting range hill, two dozen little bodies appeared. I lifted the binoculars. "Oh my god," I whispered. "Oh god," I said, pressing the binoculars toward Jamie.

Without even waiting to know what was coming, Summer yelped and jumped back into my SUV.

Jamie lifted the binoculars and took a quick look. "Is that . . . the Cub Scouts?" he asked in amazement.

I jumped into the driver's seat of Ian's truck. "We need to get Will," I called to the guys. They hopped into the back, and I hit the gas.

I sped across the bumpy field to intercept Will. When he was close, Ian and Dusty leaned down and pulled Will into the back of the truck.

"Layla, turn the truck around so we can get a line of fire on them," Jamie called.

I turned the truck, and getting it on higher ground, pulled to a stop. At once they started to fire.

"Fuck, there are like two dozen of them," Will called. "They are in the god damned weeds. I can't see a thing."

"Layla, we need your automatic," Ian yelled to me.

I shimmied through the window of the pickup cab and stood in the back. I unholstered the gun and took aim. The first child appeared in the grass. He was still in his Cub Scout uniform. Half of his face was a bloody pulp. He looked like a broken cherub. He came crashing toward us at an alarming rate.

"Layla, shoot," Ian yelled at me.

A moment later six more children emerged from the weeds. The guys shot at them but they were quick, moving swiftly toward the truck.

"Layla, shoot that fucking gun," Ian yelled at me.

I stood frozen.

"Shoot that fucking gun!" Ian screamed again.

A split-second later Jamie took the automatic from my hands. "It's all right," he whispered. Turning, he launched a barrage of bullets toward the oncoming children. They fell quickly. I backed up toward the cab. A moment later, however, I heard the horn on my SUV honking.

I looked back. At least four women were clawing at the side of my SUV. I realized then that Summer had locked herself in without the keys.

A boy grabbed at Will's leg, nearly pulling him to the ground. Dusty shot the child's brain through his ear.

I looked back at Summer. "Dammit," I swore. I pulled the Glock from the holster, climbed over the roof, down onto the hood of the truck, and set off in a sprint toward Summer.

"Layla!" Jamie called, but the children kept coming at them.

I dashed through the field toward Summer. When I got close, I whistled to draw the undead

Cub Scout moms' attention. Afraid I would hit Summer, I didn't want to shoot toward the SUV.

The women turned and lunged toward me. I was quick. I shot the first two with no problem. The second two were fast, and I missed. As the third one came close, I finally got a shot off. The fourth, however, seemed to purposefully avoid being shot. She dodged. I pulled my sword and let her get in close. I swung, decapitating her. Her head fell to the ground. The body wandered across the grass a few more steps then toppled over.

I stood over the head. It was still biting and snapping at me. I stabbed it between the eyes; the pale moons lost their sheen.

I ran toward Summer but heard rustling in the brush behind me. I turned to find a plump little red-haired boy bearing down on me. Child or not, he would kill me and eat me alive. Or worse yet, turn me into one of them.

He grunted and charged.

I pulled a dagger out of my belt and lobbed it at him. It hit him squarely between the eyes. He fell to the ground with a thud.

I looked behind me to see Ian swing into the cab of the truck. They drove back toward the SUV. In the back, the others fired shots into the weeds.

I bent low to pull my dagger from the boy's head. I pulled the dagger, sticky with blood, from his little forehead. I felt sick. I turned and retched into the weeds. It was too horrible.

I'd just caught my breath when the truck pulled up beside me. Jamie jumped out and came over to me; Will went to the SUV to check on Summer.

Jamie put his hand on my shoulder. "You okay?" he whispered.

I wiped my mouth with the back of my hand and stood up. "Yeah," I said with a heavy sigh.

"Layla, you all right?" Ian called from the truck.

I nodded.

"Come on," Jamie said. He took the dagger from my hand and cleaned it on the grass. He handed it back to me. "It's done now," he said, and we walked back to my SUV.

Will was talking to Summer, calming her.

"I'm okay now," she whispered, wiping tears. She smiled at me and shook her head in disbelief.

"This is a lot of work for a 5 gallon can of fruit cocktail," Dusty said finally, causing us all to laugh.

We loaded back into the vehicles and drove to the hunting club.

CHAPTER 12

WE KEPT A SHARP EYE on the tall grass as we headed toward the building.

"We haven't seen the Scout leaders yet," Summer observed.

Everyone's weapons were poised and ready. Will opened the door. The place was seemingly deserted. The kitchen was in a state of upheaval; brown bag lunches and puddles of blood covered the floor.

I heard Summer inhale sharply at the sight.

Bloody child-sized footprints marred the white tile floors.

"Stay close," I whispered to Summer. I holstered my gun and pulled my sword from its scabbard.

We passed through the kitchen and down a hallway toward the reception hall. At the end of the hallway, Dusty looked out.

"Eww, man, there are your Scout leaders," Dusty said.

The terrible smell of decay filled the otherwise beautiful room. On the one hand, the room boasted a massive stone fireplace with an elaborately carved mantel. Overhead, a lovely chandelier twinkled in the morning sunlight. The windows were all outlined with stained glass that depicted woodland scenes. Rays of sunlight illuminated the colored glass which cast a rainbow of sunny blotches on the floor. On the other hand, the remains of two men lay heaped on the floor. Not much was left save their skeletons and hanging bits of flesh and entrails. A small boy, about eight years of age, was chewing on the rib bone of one of the men.

Ian stepped forward and shot the undead child. The boy's head exploded, a shower of blood and bits raining onto the floor.

"There could be more," Jamie said. "Let's sweep the building. You guys take that end," he said, motioning to Dusty and Will, "Ian and I can cover this end. Summer and Layla hang here and watch outside for movement," Jamie said, and they set off in opposite directions.

I slid my belt knife off and handed it to Summer. "Keep this on you. And we need to get you a gun."

"Layla, you know I'm not . . . well, you know," she said, shaking her head as she took the knife. She stuffed it into her back pocket.

I knew exactly what she meant. Summer was a gentle girl. She used to squeal and cry when the boys teased her with worms. "Just in case," I said.

She nodded.

Will and Dusty came back.

"All clear," Will said. "Let's head to the kitchen and get started," he told Summer.

"I'll keep watch here," I said. The three of them moved off.

I couldn't see anything moving outside. I headed toward the long hallway down which Jamie and Ian had disappeared. When I reached hallway, I heard their voices. Their words were heated. I accidently caught a snippet of conversation. What I heard made me pause.

"All I'm saying is apologize, man. Not everyone can just blow a kid's brains out. You've got no business yelling at her like that," Jamie was saying.

"She knows it was just in the heat of the moment. She's fine," Ian replied.

"Christ, Ian, after everything you put her through you expect her to just pick up where you left off, with all your bullshit still intact," Jamie said.

"What the fuck is it to you, brother? What are you doing with her all the time anyway? What have *you* got on *your* mind?"

"At least I'm seeing her for who she is, not who she was. Which is more than I can say for you," Jamie replied.

"You better step off, brother. You better step off," Ian warned.

"Or what?" Jamie replied.

There was a glass door at the end of the hallway. Out of the corner of my eye, I spotted movement outside. I followed the hallway the opposite direction from where the brothers were arguing. I didn't want to hear anymore. At the end of the hallway, I leaned against the glass and looked outside. There was no one there.

I pushed the door open and went out. I looked around. There was no one, but to the right of the shooting range sat a gray wolf. It sat on the lawn looking expectantly at me. I walked down the stairs and moved slowly across the lawn toward the animal.

The wolf turned and trotted into the tall grass. I saw only its tail wagging through the tall weeds. It reappeared on the other side of the field where the grassy met the edge of the forest. It turned once more and stood looking at me. It was almost like it was waiting.

A moment later the door on the porch opened. I stood still and didn't look back. I was waiting too.

"What is it?" Jamie asked, coming up behind me.

I turned and looked. Only Jamie had come.

"A wolf, there, by the tree line," I said, pointing.

Jamie peered toward the woods.

The wolf turned and trotted into the forest.

"That's unusual," he said.

I nodded. "Let's go check out the shooting range."

Jamie walked silently beside me. I could tell he was thinking, and I really hoped he didn't know I'd overheard their argument. Embarrassed, I felt like a snoop.

We rounded the earthen wall and walked down the steps to the shooting stand.

"Booyah," Jamie said.

There, laid out on the tables at the shooting stand, was row after row of guns and ammo.

"They must have been doing hunter's safety training or something," I said as we walked amongst the tables, picking up the rifles.

"I don't know what they were doing, but I sure am glad," Jamie said. "Come on, let's get the others," he added, and we headed back.

Jamie went to pull the SUV closer to the range, and I went inside to get some help. As I walked toward the kitchen, I heard Summer and Ian talking.

"Your reception was so beautiful. You remember the cake? Mom and I almost dropped it carrying it up those back steps," Summer was telling Ian.

They both chuckled.

"Yeah, it really was beautiful. You and your mom really did a great job," Ian replied.

A lump rose in my throat.

I walked into the kitchen just as Dusty and Ian exited the storage cupboard pushing dollies with boxes of food. I smiled. "You think that's a good haul, wait until you see what we found out back," I said.

We finished loading Ian's truck with the cases of canned foods then headed around back to the shooting range where Jamie had been loading my SUV. We loaded all the guns and ammo. Inside, we'd also found several more cases of ammo. Though it had been a rough go, the haul was worth it.

It was after noon when we left Mara Hunting Club. Jamie and Will rode in the back of Ian's truck keeping the supplies secure while Summer and Dusty took my SUV. I rode back with Ian. As we pulled away from the club, I looked in the rear view mirror. The wolf appeared again at the edge of the forest.

Ian turned the truck toward town. The image of the wolf fell out of sight. We'd been riding in silence for a long time before Ian finally reached out and took my hand.

"Hey, sorry I yelled at you today," he said, squeezing my fingers.

I nodded but pulled my hand back.

I looked in the mirror again to find Jamie looking at me. Caught, he smiled abashedly. I smiled and winked playfully at him. Then we headed home.

CHAPTER 13

WHEN I WAS FIFTEEN, IAN AND I had snuck away from my grandma and his parents at the Fourth of July fireworks display to make out under the bridge. I remembered seeing, as we snuck off in the darkness, the townspeople in Grandin Park looking upward as fireworks exploded. Their faces were illuminated shades of green, yellow, and pink in the exploding light. I remembered my grandmother's face clearest of all. How happy she'd seemed, her face glowing pink, as she delighted in the simple things of life.

Standing on the street in front of the bridge, I turned and looked behind me. Almost everyone had come. The remaining townspeople were assembled in Grandin Park to watch the newest fireworks display. Sadness and despair wracked every face. People looked like pale, hollow versions of themselves. Everyone shifted nervously. They wouldn't miss this sight for the world but were in fear of their lives every second.

Larry appeared from under the bridge and signaled for everyone to get back. I jogged back toward the park and waited with the others. Larry made a few adjustments to the fuse box and then, with a quick movement, set something alight and ran to join us.

"Cover your ears," Jamie said to me.

Moments later a noise, much like a fireworks finale, sounded. I felt the ground shake under me. We covered our ears and ducked. The old metal bridge groaned. Asphalt flew into the air then dropped into the river below. A huge puff of smoke enveloped the structure, and with a heave, the middle of the Hamletville Bridge began to collapse. There was an awful grinding sound as the bridge seemed to resist its destruction. Finally, the beams gave way, and the structure fell apart in the middle, the pieces falling into the river.

"She's down," Larry called.

"I feel like we just destroyed civilization," I whispered to Jamie, fighting back tears.

I turned to look behind me. The residents, their faces long and pale, had already turned away and headed back to whatever they had left.

The death of the bridge ensured our survival. With the bridge collapsed, there was no way the undead could reach the town from the interstate — unless they decided to swim — which was the main route into our town. The barricades at either end of

Main Street were now in place. A mess of old vehicles, scrap metal, farm equipment, and barbed wire and fencing ran cross the road and between buildings at either end of town. The town entryways were now secure enough to slow any visitors. All of us were poignantly aware that there were many farms scattered across the countryside with bodies yet unaccounted for; some visitors were expected. Otherwise there was the wildness of the forest and the dark black waves of the lake to protect us. With the bridge down, there was a certain finality to the entire situation.

We spent the next three weeks canvasing the town to rid it of pesky undead locked in houses and raiding residents' homes for supplies. Everything was stored in the elementary school gym. We decided to work on an honors system: take only what you need. We made arrangements to rotate shifts at the school and the barricades. Everyone was accounted for and paired up to be protected. And everyone was acutely aware we'd had absolutely no contact from the outside. Thus far Kiki had no luck with the radio. The world, it seemed, had gone silent. It was something we knew but did not talk about. We were alone.

Around mid-October, Fred noticed that Tander Vineyard and Orchard looked ready to bust at its seams. A popular spot for passing tourists, the Tander Orchard usually offered fruit picking, a pumpkin patch, and hayrides every autumn. Fred Johnson had checked the Tander house, but the family was nowhere to be found. We all decided to head out one morning and collect the harvest. Ethel had arranged to show us all how to do canning and had a workshop set up in the gym. We had begun to function like an authentic village.

Jamie and Fred drove tractors with attached wagons to the farm that morning. Jamie had convinced a reluctant Frenchie to bring the girls. It took some doing. They almost never left the cabin. I didn't blame Frenchie. If they were my children, I would have stayed put as well.

I rode with Jamie, Frenchie, and the girls in the wagon. The girls were very excited. It was a chilly fall morning. The first freeze had not yet come, but it was close. The scene looked almost like a tailgate party. There were about two dozen people there, most of them armed. Empty bushel baskets sat on the ground.

Ian and Tom approached us when we arrived.

"Swept the entire place. Looks clear," Ian said.

"We've got armed folks all around the farm keeping an eye out," Tom added.

"I want a pumpkin," Kira squealed.

"Me too," Susan called.

"Let's go," Tom said. He picked Kira up and swung her onto his shoulders.

Frenchie, hand in hand with Susan, smiled at me and followed Tom.

I grinned at her.

April, Summer, Ethel, Jensen, and Larry pulled up in Larry's van.

Ethel emerged with a large box. "Until I figure out how to bake in a fire pit, this will have to do," she said. "I used Mrs. Winchester's recipe for homemade granola. Got it a bit burnt I'm afraid, and I think I used up the last raisins on the planet," she said and started handing out small bags to all of us.

Jamie took a bag and kissed Ethel on the cheek. "You're an angel," he said.

Ethel pinched his cheek. "Honey, that's you. How come you never got married? Summer, why don't you go with Jamie?"

Summer looked like she wanted to sink into the ground. "Good lord, mother, the apocalypse is here and you're still trying to fix me up."

Everyone chuckled.

"Oh, there's Frenchie and her girls. I have something special for them. Let's go," Ethel said, pulling Summer behind her. Summer shook her head and rolled her eyes as she passed me.

"Tom's got people working the vines and the pumpkins. A few people are back in the cherry orchard. We still need people to pick apples. I thought we could work up here," Ian told Jamie, April, and me.

We all picked up some baskets and headed into the orchard. Ian, his gun slung over his shoulder, kept watch. It was a beautiful morning. The sky was clear. The hardwood trees had lost most of their leaves. The remaining foliage, now drab brown, rust, and deep red in color, was about to drop. The apple trees were thick with fruit. The fallen apples filled the air with the tangy smell of decayed fruit. Yellow jackets buzzed the apples.

April was working in the tree next to mine. I could hear her and Ian chatting. I wondered what kind of relationship they'd developed over the last four years. April and Kristie had always been very close.

I filled the first basket of apples and headed back to the wagon with my load. The bushel was surprisingly heavy. Jamie was on his way back to the orchard when he intercepted me.

"Here, let me take that for you," he said, taking the bushel from my hands.

"Got to help the little lady, huh?"

He laughed. "I'm sure you can handle it. I'm just being gentlemanly. Didn't you hear Ethel? I'm a great catch."

I looked up at Jamie. I'd never noticed before how different his eyes were from Ian's. I knew they both had blue eyes, but Jamie's eyes were a deeper shade, the blue intermixed with flecks of green and gold. I smiled at him. "What happened with that girl from Sparkstown?"

Jamie shrugged. "That ended a couple of years ago. She was nothing special."

"Well, you'll be hard-pressed now," I said.

"Hard-pressed for what?"

"To find someone special."

Jamie lowered the apple bushel into the wagon. He looked at me and gave me a very awkward smile. "I don't know about that."

Just then a truck pulled into the farm, music blaring loudly. Jeff.

"Hey man, you want every undead asshole left in the county following you here? Turn it down," Jamie told him as he approached Jeff's truck window.

Jeff got out of the truck carrying an oversized CD player. He put it on his shoulder; "Just like the 80s, right?" he said and danced his way to the back of his truck. He dropped the tailgate. There he had stashed three large coolers. Within, bottles of beer swam in cold lake water. "Want one?" he asked.

Jamie shook his head.

"It's a bit early," I said.

"Well, considering I might die tomorrow, I'm not really watching the clock," he replied as he cracked open a bottle.

"But you can get to work," I said, handing an empty basket to him, "if you want to eat."

"Thought I might try a liquid diet," he said, lifting the bottle and looking at it in the sunlight. "Just kidding, Layla. I'll get going in a minute," he said and took the basket from me.

I was just grabbing myself another basket when Tom returned.

"Jamie, can you take the tractor back to the field? They're ready to load the gourds and pumpkins."

Ian joined us.

"Sure," Jamie said with a nod. The old tractor kicked on with a lurch. With a wave, Jamie pulled away.

I grabbed a ladder and headed back to finish the top of the tree I was working on. I waved to April. She was hoisting the long fruit picker, a kind of clawed basket at the end of a long pole, into the top of a tree near mine. She smiled, half-tolerantly, at me.

I popped open the ladder and climbed up. When I got halfway up, two things became apparent: I needed to use the shoulder sling to collect the apples, and my sword and holster were in the way. I climbed back down, hung my scabbard strap on the top of the ladder, and swung the holster from a bottom limb. Donning the shoulder sling, I climbed back up the ladder and started loading apples into the satchel. I paused to eat a perfect-looking fruit. Its skin was mostly green but was blushed red. The sweet and tart juices filled my mouth.

In the distance I could see Jeff and Ian sitting on Jeff's tailgate. They were both drinking. Jeff had turned the music back on. It wasn't loud, but I could hear the beat of the rock music from where I was perched.

I had already filled my satchel halfway when I could no longer reach the apples from my ladder. Grabbing a thick branch, I pulled myself up into the tree. Once I was perched near the top, I took a break to stretch my back. The sun was high in the sky now; I was starting to sweat. The bugs were becoming particularly annoying. I stopped, pulled the small canteen off my belt, and took a long drink. I looked for April to offer her some water when I saw someone standing very near my tree. I could not make out the person well through the leaves, but every hair on the back of my neck rose. The person stood there saying nothing. They just stood. I knew then who—or what—it was.

It had not yet seen me. I cursed myself in every language I knew. My guns and sword were out of reach. I slowly pulled my feet up and slid the poyasni from my boots.

"Ouch. Dammit. God-damned yellow jackets," April cursed.

The figure under me moved. Then I saw three others. They all closed in on her.

"April, watch out!" I screamed.

The one who had stood under my tree turned then and came back. He jogged around the bottom of my tree trying to catch sight of me. He was joined a moment later by another undead man. They both swung at me, trying to pull me from the tree.

April screamed and tried to run, swinging the apple picker at the undead men who tried to grab her.

"Ian!" I screamed at the top of my lungs. "Ian, help!"

Larry and Jensen had just got back to the truck. They were setting their bushels down.

"Ian!" I screamed louder. "Larry!"

The undead men bumped against the ladder knocking it and my weapons on the ground.

"Layla, help!" April screamed. She was trying to climb into the tree but they were grabbing at her.

I swung down, trying to strike one of the undead with a dagger. They were out of range, and my position was too awkward. I could neither throw nor strike. I considered jumping out of the tree but landing would be clumsy and slow. I was about to try anyway when April let out a blood curdling cry.

The men looked up. "Ian, help!!" I screamed again, waving at him. He saw me then. Dropping everything, the men took off in a sprint, weapons drawn.

Through the leaves I saw April had been pulled to the ground. She was screaming but still kicking and fighting.

Moments later there was gunfire. The undead figures hovering over April fell to the ground. I heard April crying and moaning.

They shot the two undead under my tree. As soon as they hit the ground I clambered out of the tree, grabbed my weapons, and ran to April.

We were too late. One of her sneakers had been torn off, and her foot was badly wounded. She had been bitten. Her leg was bleeding profusely.

"Someone get Jamie," I said as I pulled on a pair of medical gloves.

Jensen took off in a sprint.

I cursed myself for my carelessness, cursed myself because April had no hope. I slid the gloves on and taking my knife, cut away April's jeans. A nasty bite wound was revealed.

"Oh no, no, no," April moaned.

Ian took April's hand.

My hands shook. Larry pulled off his belt and handed it to me. I wrapped the belt around April's leg and pulled it tight. She moaned.

Jensen and Jamie came running up. "God dammit, Ian. I told you to keep an eye on . . . them," he cursed and dropped to his knees. "Go get everyone rounded up and sweep this place again," he told his brother angrily as he pulled on his gloves.

Ian rose and walked off.

"Music probably attracted them," I said quietly as Jamie looked April over.

He nodded, but I could see he was angry. "Are you okay?" he asked.

"Yeah."

"Oh, oh God, oh no," April groaned.

I handed Jamie my canteen, and he poured water over April's foot and leg. It washed the blood away. We could see then that the blood around the bite marks had already started to coagulate. The veins in her legs turned dark blue, and her skin grew pale. We watched, horrified, as the rosy glow of her skin faded as the contamination spread. From the bite on her foot up her leg, the skin slowly lost its pigment. Her skin faded pale white as the diseased blood traveled up her body. Moments later she went silent. She stiffened for a moment then jerked spasmodically as the infection climbed across her face. Her skin bleached white, the veins in her forehead darkening. She jerked several more times then became still. She was moon white. Her veins, evident under her flesh, were dark blue. Her eyes fluttered closed.

How different. I heard April's voice in my head. Again she repeated: *how different.*

I looked around. Clearly, no one else had heard her. Jensen, Jeff, and Larry were looking down at April. Jamie and I rose. We all stared down at April's body. She lay in the tall green grass. Purple violets made a halo around her. No one breathed.

We heard a gunshot in the distance followed by two more.

A moment later, April sat up. She opened her eyes and looked at us. Her eyes had gone pale white with the now-familiar streaks of red. Frothy saliva began to drop from the corner of her mouth.

Jensen raised his gun.

April turned to look at him.

No, I heard like a whisper in the wind.

Jensen pulled the trigger. April fell back. A spray of blood and brains covered the grass.

Ian ran back up to us. "There were two more out there. It was the Tanders and their boys. Maybe two farm workers. Looks like the place is clear now," he said. He looked down at April.

I watched the expression on his face change. It was as if he'd just realized what had happened. It occurred to me then how careless Ian was with other people's lives. I looked away from him.

"Let's get the bodies cleared, get April buried, and finish the job," I said.

Solemnly, everyone nodded. Clouds rolled in, occluding the sun. The wind whipped hard. There was a bitter chill in the air. Ian knelt beside April.

Jamie turned and headed back to the tractor. He pulled off his gloves and dashed them to the ground. The men moved off behind him. I looked up at the sky. A hawk passed overhead. I turned and followed Jamie.

CHAPTER 14

BY THE END OF OCTOBER, the first snow began to fall. Though apple picking had ended in tragedy, the bounty reaped lasted a long time. Ethel had us all cranking out apple sauce and canning vegetables. In addition, Grandma's house yielded a treasure trove of supplies from the mundane, like rice and sugar, to the more exotic, like Kevlar vests and a stash of board games for children. We were ready to begin our hibernation.

Mother Nature determined she would not make things any easier on us. When winter arrived, it was clear it meant to stay. The *Farmer's Almanac* predicted a harsh winter. Lake effect weather dropped feet of snow on us. It was good on the one hand because it seemed unlikely the undead could get far in the deep snow. On the other hand, we were going through wood at such an alarming rate that we had to adjust our habits. There would be no more comfortable nights roaming about the cozy cabin. Frenchie, the girls, and I had taken to wearing at least three layers at all times and lived most of our life in the living room in front of the fireplace. We spent the next several weeks in quiet hibernation.

On Thanksgiving morning, however, Jamie came by. He decided we *needed* turkey. That meant, of course, a hunting trip was in order. Ian, who planned to come by later, was due for a rotation in town so that left Jamie and me with the task of hunting down a Thanksgiving feast. We left at the crack of dawn.

"How long does it take for a human body to decompose?" I asked Jamie as we hiked through the shin-deep snow into the forest behind Grandma's house.

There was a fresh snowfall that morning leaving a powdery, sand-like layer of snow on top of already accumulated inches. In the early morning sunlight, the snow picked up a prism of rainbow colors. It was peaceful and quiet in the woods save for the swishing sounds of our feet in the snow and our chatter.

"Now what makes you think I would know that?" he replied.

"Seems like something a medic should know."

He chuckled. "I think it takes a year if the body is exposed to the elements. If it's in a grave or a house or something like that, it will take longer. Depends on the environment."

"Then, theoretically, by spring there could just be a bunch of rattling skeletons walking around."

"That's a pretty gruesome image," Jamie replied.

"No worse than a rotting corpse walking around."

"True," he replied then motioned me to be silent. "There," he whispered, pointing to some fresh turkey tracks in the snow. He looked around. "I bet they are in the field picking at the wheat," he whispered.

The tracks on the ground seemed to lead two directions—toward the field and toward a thicket of mountain laurel.

"I'll check there if you want to check the field," I offered, pointing to the thicket.

"Sure, just watch your ass—which looks cute in those Carharts by the way—and yell if you see anything."

Flashing him a smile, I rolled my eyes, and we went off in different directions.

Jamie passed over a rise toward the field, and I followed the turkey tracks toward the thicket. After I'd gone a short ways, the tracks disappeared. I looked up into the pines to see if they had roosted, but I couldn't see them anywhere, and I was not much of a tracker. I turned to go when movement coming from the thicket caught my attention.

I snapped the safety off the hunting rifle and knelt in the snow.

A moment later, an albino doe appeared from the thicket. It was munching on the small tufts of grass that stuck up through the drifts. It moved peacefully. It was an amazingly beautiful creature. Its white pelt melted into the surroundings, the pink around its crystal blue eyes, nose, and inner-ear looking almost cheerful in the snowy landscape. It moved off. Intrigued, I followed.

The doe moved away from the path we'd been following and deeper into the woods. I looked behind me to ensure I could follow my tracks; they were easy to see. The deer occasionally stopped and looked at me. It did not seem to fear me and, in fact, looked rather inquisitively toward me. Something about the creature made all the hairs on the back of my neck rise. She led and I followed. She trotted deeper into the woods, into an area I did not know well. Here the trees grew very tall and thick. Once we entered, I had a hard time following her. She disappeared behind the wide trunks of the oak trees. I made turn after turn, catching glimpses of her as she wound deeper into the forest. The snow seemed even more luminescent here. The hemlock trees were covered in crystal-like snow and glowed iridescently. The limbs of the large oaks were hung with glittering icicles.

At last I saw her again. She stood in a small space between two hemlocks, the trees bending above her like an arching doorway. She turned and entered the space.

My heart raced. I followed.

Passing through the hemlocks, I found myself standing in a small circular clearing. The entire space was ringed with massive oak trees. The place was incredibly pristine white and everything shimmered. Standing in the middle of this space was a very tall and elegant looking man and woman. They both wore white robes trimmed with fox fur and moonstones. The man had long, ebony colored hair and wore a crown that looked like the horns of a stag. The woman had flowing blonde hair that was almost white in color. She had large, doe-shaped eyes that twinkled.

The man beckoned kindly toward me.

I was frozen in place.

He turned and smiled at the woman. She extended one hand toward me. In that hand she held a crown of holly. She smiled invitingly.

I took a step forward.

"Layla!" a voice screamed in the far off distance.

A look passed between the magisterial man and woman.

"Layla!"

I recognized Jamie's voice then and the urgency and fear in it. Stunned, I realized he might be under attack.

I turned then, not looking back, and headed away from the pair. I stamped back over my footsteps, cursing myself for foolishness when another person's life depended on me. I ran, my heart bursting in my chest, to get to Jamie. If anything happened to him, if I lost him, I could not forgive myself. The weight of the idea, of the thought that Jamie could be hurt, hit me hard.

Moments later I found myself back at the thicket where the doe had appeared.

Jamie looked frantic and was calling my name.

"Here, here!" I yelled, relieved to see that he was all right.

"Thank god," he said, dropping the birds he'd been holding. I hadn't even heard the gunshots. He grabbed me tightly, squeezing me against his chest. "Where the hell did you go? I couldn't find your tracks anywhere. Didn't you hear me calling you?"

I shook my head. "No, I was just—" I began then stopped. I was just what? What would I say? It was one thing for Grandma Petrovich to have her eccentricities. It was quite another for me to go around seeing things. "I got lost."

Jamie kissed the top of my head. "Oh Layla, please never do that to me again," he whispered.

I looked up at him. Our eyes met and something inside me saw Jamie in a much different light. I realized then it was a feeling that had been growing all this time. With Ian in the picture, my feelings were confused. Now, staring up at Jamie, I was clear. One thing was very certain; I wanted to kiss him.

He leaned in and set the sweetest, lightest kiss on my lips. "Layla," he whispered, brushing his hand against my cheek and down my hair.

I didn't resist. I kissed him back and this time caught the sweet taste of his mouth. It was unlike anything I had ever experienced in a kiss before. His mouth had a natural sweetness, like the light taste of raw honey. His lips, his body's chemistry, were sweeter than any I'd known before.

We pulled back and smiled goofily at one another.

He kissed me on my forehead. "Two turkeys, not just one," he said and picked up the birds, "and what did you get?" he asked with joking competitiveness.

The image of the pale woman and her extended crown fluttered through my head. I smiled at him. Taking my glove off, I touched my hand to his lips. "You," I replied.

He smiled and kissed my fingers. "I like your answer better," he said and then, slinging the birds over his shoulder, took my hand, and we turned back toward the cabin. "Hmm, who do you think will win the game tonight?" he asked jokingly.

"Well, Team Undead seems to be having a great season," I replied.

We both laughed and headed back to the cabin hand in hand.

CHAPTER 15

THAT NIGHT I LAY AWAKE, restless. The puzzle of the man and woman in the woods stuck with me. I remembered that my grandmother had mentioned that forest spirits lived in the woods behind our house. Is that what I had seen? Forest spirits? Memories of old folktales floated through my mind, a kaleidoscope of different cultures. What, exactly, had I seen? And what, exactly, had they wanted from me? Part of me wondered if I had hallucinated the whole exchange. I knew, however, that whatever Grandma had done to me before the pandemic hit, her special tea, had changed me forever.

It was nearly two in the morning when I heard a snowmobile pull up outside the cabin. Ian had been missing all day. Even though we'd asked him to join us, he did not come for dinner. Part of me hoped he'd simply stayed in town.

Our dinner had been perfect. We used the old spit in the fireplace to roast the turkeys, and Jamie and Frenchie made a meal out of canned goods.

Kira and Susan had looked truly happy, and I didn't blame them. I also felt the happiest I had felt in years. Jamie played board games with the girls all night, giving me goofy and bashful smiles from time to time. Each time he did, I just wanted to scoop him into my arms and hug him until the world ended — again. I offered Jamie my spare room for the night. He was sleeping, snoring loudly, in Grandma's old sewing room.

The front door opened and shut. I heard Ian slide the bars and locks closed. A few minutes later I heard him banking up the logs in the fireplace. I lay in bed and tried to sleep. After half an hour, the whole house felt incredibly warm. I slid out of bed. Checking on Jamie and Frenchie and her girls, I found everyone else was asleep. In the living room, Ian was sitting in front of a roaring fire. The temperature in the living room was ghastly hot. His head was bowed. He held a bottle of beer loosely in one hand.

"I thought you didn't like warm beer," I whispered, taking the bottle from his fingers, setting it on the side table.

He looked up at me and smiled, but I could tell right away that all was not well.

"What's wrong?"

He shook his head. "Nothing, I'm just not feeling great. I've been having bouts off and on for the last year or so. I just feel off, some pain in my stomach," he said.

"Is it an ulcer?" I asked. I kneeled on the floor and opened the chimney flue to let some of the warm air out.

Surprising me, he took my hand. "I think so."

"What did the doctor say?" I pulled my hand back.

"Nothing. I never went. We couldn't afford it."

The *we* in the sentence hung in the air. I put my hand on his forehead. "No fever. You feel cold?"

He nodded.

Trying to make as little noise as possible, I went into the kitchen and grabbed a teapot. I set the water on to boil in the fireplace. After a few minutes I could hear the water rolling inside the pot. I moved it from the heat before it could whistle and made Ian a cup of tea. He smiled at me and sipped it slowly.

"I think we need to call a town meeting," he said after a while. "The lake is frozen over, and the river is starting to jam with ice. I think people are feeling isolated, and at two houses I stopped at today, people had the flu. They were worried they had whatever killed everyone else, but Mrs. Finch thought it was just seasonal flu."

"It might not be good to get everyone together if people are getting sick."

"They could wear masks and gloves."

"Let's wait and make sure the flu passes. Don't want to risk it. Unless there is an emergency, maybe we should just call everyone for a New Year's celebration. After all, we did live."

"That's a good idea. We could even get out some of the old prom gear from the school storage, make it a party," Ian added. He smiled at me. "Remember our prom?"

"How can I forget? Poor Grandma, bless her heart, wherever did she find that terrible yellow prom gown? I didn't have the heart to tell I wouldn't wear it."

"I remember they called you Big Bird, but you looked beautiful to me," he said and smiled. "Hey, you still have that dress?"

"I 'm not sure I want to answer that question."

"You should wear it again. Some people might get a kick out of it."

"Some people?"

"Well, me."

"I am not sure I want to open myself up to that kind of ridicule again."

Ian set the cup down. He took my hands, stroking my fingers. "That was the best night of my life," he whispered. We looked at one another. We both knew it was the night we'd made love for the first time.

"Jesus," Jamie said as he ambled sleepily into the living room, "why the hell is it so hot in here?" He stopped and looked down at us.

I pulled my hands away, but I was too late.

"What the hell are you doing back so late?" Jamie scolded his brother.

Ian looked puzzled.

I lowered my eyes.

"I was all over town today. People are getting sick. You probably need to get out there and check on folks tomorrow."

"Yeah, yeah, I guess I better do that. Doesn't look like I'm much needed here anyway," he said and turned to go back to bed. "Stoke down the fire, Layla, you're letting it get too hot," he called as he walked out of the room. The edge in his voice was clear, but his meaning hit me even harder.

"What's with him?" Ian asked.

I shrugged. "Well, I'm going back to bed now. You're okay?" I asked and rose.

"Good enough, I guess," he said. "Goodnight," he added, gazing up at me. The look on his face told me what he was wishing for. I had seen that look many times in the past.

"Goodnight," I replied simply and walked down the hall.

Before I went to bed, I paused in the hallway outside the spare room. I didn't hear Jamie snoring.

"Jamie?" I whispered.

He didn't answer me, but I knew he was awake.

"It wasn't what it looked like," I whispered into the darkness. "I'm not—I don't want—Jamie?"

Still he did not reply.

Sighing, I went back to my bed and lay down. I was just dozing off to sleep when someone sat down on the bed beside me. I worried about who had come.

I opened my eyes and tried to focus in the dim light. I found my grandmother looking down at me.

"Grandma?" I said too loudly, clambering to sit up.

She lifted her finger to her lips to silence me and motioned for me to stay comfortable.

"What is it?" I whispered.

My darling, she said to me, *be brave, but be aware too. The great eye within you is open, but you need to see. Make sure you see, Layla, really see.*

"See what?" I whispered.

Everything, she said with a smile then faded. *See everything.*

CHAPTER 16

BY CHRISTMAS EVE THE FLU had run through the town and killed twelve of the elderly citizens, including Mr. Franklin. The flu provided Jamie with a good excuse to stay away from me. I almost never saw him, and when I did, he pretended nothing had happened—neither the kiss nor his jealousy. It was as if he erased the whole moment in the woods from his memory, and we'd gone back to being friends and only friends. The more he acted, the angrier I became. I didn't want to be his friend. I wanted him.

On Christmas Eve day, I dragged home a small pine tree for the girls.

"Oh, look at this!" Susan screamed excitedly.

"Grandma made me toss the Christmas ornaments, but I thought we could make some decorations ourselves," I told the girls as I set up the tree.

The last few months had been hard on the little girls I'd come to love so dearly. They had both lost too much weight and many times they were sad and sulking. They had seen too much.

We rifled around the house and found a bunch of miscellaneous items to make decorations: empty shotgun shells, canning rings, and other small items. I'd unearthed some silver paint from the barn. Frenchie put the excited children to work painting then pulled me into the kitchen.

"I have nothing for them," she whispered, distressed.

"I was going to head into town really quick. I needed to run an errand. Don't worry, I'll find something. Lend me your credit card?"

She laughed. "Thank you."

I reloaded the guns and went out to the barn and got on the snowmobile. It was bitterly cold. I had on my heavy winter jacket and goggles. The snowmobile purred when I started it. After securing the cabin, I headed down the snow-covered road toward town.

It was eerie to see the town completely deserted and covered in deep snow. If anyone else had been around, it was not apparent. The snow had drifted everywhere. I stopped first at the grocery store. While we had cleared the place of food and daily living supplies, I remembered that the owners had a claw machine full of toys.

I pulled my gun and pushed the door open. "Anyone inside?" I called. "I don't want to shoot you, unless you're already dead."

After a moment had passed with no answer and no movement, I went inside. The large windows of the grocery store illuminated the space. We'd already cleared the store out, but you could never be too careful. That was a lesson I'd learned once too often. The shelves of the store were nearly bare. We'd cleared the store of rotting food to ensure it didn't become a germ pool. Miscellaneous items littered the shelves, but the essentials were gone. At the back of the store I found the claw machine. Inside were numerous dolls, stuffed animals, and packs of plastic toys. Not wanting to break the glass and get shards on the toys, I pondered what to do. I pushed the machine from the wall then grabbed the axe that hung by the fire extinguisher near the back door. With a heave, I chopped the lock. After two swings the case opened. I grabbed the nicest toys I could find and stuffed them into my backpack.

I was on my way out, moving through the aisles, when I heard the front door bang open.

I ducked low. I held the gun in one hand and the axe in the other. I crept down the aisle, keeping an eye out for feet, and listened for movement. Nothing. I made my way to the end of the aisle.

"Anyone alive out there?" I called.

There was no answer. The door squeaked on its hinges as it wagged back and forth in the bitter cold wind.

I stepped out into the main aisle. There was a figure at the end of the row. Startled, I shot. A moment later I realized I was standing across from a cardboard cutout of Orville Redenbacher. I'd shot the popcorn aficionado between the eyes. Not a bad shot.

The wind blew hard outside. I walked over to the door. The only tracks leading in were mine. Blaming the wind and jumpy nerves, I pulled the door firmly shut and used the axe to secure the handle.

I then headed across the street to the only boutique in town. The front door was still locked so I headed around the back. The heavy metal back door pulled open with a heave.

"Customer at the back. I need a fitting," I called.

Nothing.

Pulling the door firmly shut behind me, I went inside. The atmosphere of the store was a bittersweet contrast to our new world. It was like someone had hit the pause button on modern life. Kiki's mother Lil had opened the small boutique a few years back. She'd decorated the place in faux Italian style with antiqued wall paint, gold filigree chairs, and images of the Italian countryside on the walls. Inside I found a mix of clothes; house gowns for the seniors, homecoming gowns for the teens, and practical attire for men and women. I looked around the store and considered my options. At last, I selected heavy wool sweaters for Frenchie and Ian. I also spotted a number of prom tiaras in a glass case. I grabbed two of them for the little princesses. I stuffed all the items into my backpack. As I was exiting, I caught a glimpse of myself in a full-length mirror. It made me stop.

"Christ, I look like Mad Max," I muttered. Well, a cross between Mad Max and an Eskimo. This would never do.

I set the bag down and went to the clothing racks. There I found a black cashmere sweater. I pulled it off the cloth hanger. Across the room Lil had undergarments. I pulled my coat off. Underneath I was wearing a stained and ripped old gray sweatshirt with a white t-shirt and sports bra underneath. I tossed them in the garbage. I stood shivering. I took a black satin camisole from the rack and slid it on. Over that I slipped on the soft sweater. At the counter Lil had perfume and make-up. I picked up a brush and smoothed my hair back, pulling it into a tight—not even a snowmobile can undo this—braid. Spraying myself with a little perfume and putting on some lipstick, I decided I looked much more feminine. I pulled my heavy winter jacked back on and headed out.

I then made my final stop, picking up the last item I wanted from Fisherman's Wharf, a small restaurant that sat lakeside. After, I drove across town to Jamie's house. It was late afternoon. The sun was just beginning to dip toward the horizon. Jamie's small stone cabin was nestled in a deep lot surrounded by white-barked Birch trees. Dim light showed through the slats in the front window. The chimney puffed a small trail of smoke. When he didn't open the door when I drove up, I was not sure what to think. Maybe Jamie was not home. Or maybe I was not welcome.

I pulled the snowmobile up to the front porch steps. Trudging through the deep snow, I went to the front door. Jamie did not answer when I knocked. I peeked through the window. He had a gas lamp burning inside. There was a book and a plate of food sitting beside the recliner. I felt worried. I knocked again.

"Jamie?" I called.

There was no answer, but I thought I heard movement inside. Hedging my bets, I tried the door. It was unlocked. Now I was really worried. I pushed the door open and entered.

"Jamie?" I called again.

After a moment, Jamie called a weak "here," from the back of the house. I pulled my boots and coat off and followed the hallway to the back. It was cold inside. I found Jamie in the bathroom leaning over the tub. He was vomiting into a bucket.

Every muscle on my body seized tight.

"It's just the flu. I promise," he said.

I grabbed a towel off the shelf and headed back to the kitchen where I had spotted some bottled water. I went back to the bathroom, wetted the towel, and wiped Jamie's face. I handed him the water. "Drink a little," I encouraged.

He turned, his back against the tub, knees propped, and drank.

"How long have you been sick?" I asked, mopping his face.

"A few days," he replied. "Should be out of the woods by tomorrow."

"Why didn't you tell me?"

"I'll text you next time," he said. I could tell by his tone he was exhausted.

"Ok, big man, let's get you to bed." I offered my hands to pull him up. I put my arm around his back, draping his arm across my shoulder, and walked him down the hallway to his bedroom.

"You smell beautiful," he whispered as we walked, "and this sweater is something else," he added, "so soft."

I smiled but said nothing even though my heart was bursting.

I helped him climb into bed then raided his closet for more blankets. Back in the living room, I banked up the fire. "You got more wood outside?" I called.

"Yeah," he replied weakly.

I pulled my coat and boots back on and headed out. His wood was covered with a blue tarp at one side of the house. I brought in several loads, enough to keep him for the next couple of days.

By the time I was done the house was toasty. I made a pot of broth in an old copper kettle and set it to keep warm by the fire. I was pretty sure I couldn't mess up broth. I cleared the mess from his living room and bathroom, wiping down the entire place with anti-bacterial wipes, then headed back to check on him. He was sleeping soundly. I pulled the covers up to his chin and checked his forehead. No fever. He did not wake, and he looked very peaceful. I went back to the front, grabbing more bottled water and his oil lamp, and set them at his bedside.

I cast an eye outside; it was almost dark, and I needed to get back. I didn't want to wake him nor did I want to leave him. I sat, indecisive, at the side of his bed. I stared down at him and stroked his hair. The setting sun cast a soft pink glow on him. "See," my grandmother had told me. "See everything." I stared down at Jamie and in that moment I knew two things: first, I knew I loved Jamie, and second, I knew that knowing who I really loved was not the only thing my grandmother had wanted me to see. At last I decided I couldn't stay any longer. It was now dark, which made it dangerous to be out, and I had to make sure that Santa came for the girls.

Before I left, I set a small package on the pillow beside him. For lack of better wrapping, I had placed my gift inside one of Fisherman's Wharf's dark blue napkins. I kissed Jamie on the forehead then went outside, locking the door firmly behind me.

I hopped on the snowmobile and headed back across town. I took a shortcut through a field near the Fletchers' farm. As I crossed, I saw something strange in the middle of the field. In the dim light, I saw a figure standing waist-deep in the snow. I turned the snowmobile toward it. The headlight of the snowmobile revealed it was one of the undead. I pulled to a stop as I approached him. It was bitterly cold, the temperature well below zero. The creature was frozen in the snow, but little by little, it was forcing itself to turn and face me. Its arms seemed to have been frozen into position. With great effort, it turned its head just slightly to look at me. I could hear it make a sound like a breath.

I recognized Clark, the boy who'd helped me at the grocery store the day I'd arrived. His skin was frozen stiff, but I could still make out his face. Clark lived down by the lake. What was he doing out here?

I unzipped my jacket just enough to pull the gun from its holster. I shivered as the wind hit me and wished for a moment I still had on my old sweatshirt.

"Sorry, Clark," I said, and taking aim, I shot him in the head, sending frozen chunks of blood and brains onto the snow. They fell like crimson colored petals on the pure white canvas. Clark's body, though momentarily rocked by the gunshot, remained frozen in place.

I holstered the gun. I wondered if Santa was fighting his way through the undead this year as well. But even as I thought it, my joke seemed crude and left me feeling guilty. Clark was a nice kid. He didn't deserve to die like that. Maybe I'd become just a frozen on the inside as him. I turned the snowmobile and headed home.

Back at the cabin, I stashed the sweaters for Ian and Frenchie then handed my backpack full of gifts to Frenchie who smiled thankfully at me. The girls were excited to show me their Christmas tree ornaments. The small pine tree glimmered in the firelight. Their sweet, creative minds had made a masterpiece out of a trash pile.

"Beautiful, just beautiful," I whispered to them, kissing each on the cheek.

"Ohh, this is nice," Susan said, feeling the cashmere sweater.

"This too," Kira said, running her hand across the smooth black satin camisole that stuck out of the back of my pants.

"Okay girls," Frenchie said. She eyed me over. "Make-up too," she observed, "and perfume. You do look nice. Now, question is, where did you go?" she asked with a grin.

"Where do you think?"

"If you're using your head, then I know where you went."

"Mommy, you're funny. Layla always uses her head. It's right here," Kira said, patting me on the top of my head.

"There's your answer," I said with a laugh.

The next morning I woke to the best sound I had heard in months: the girl's excited laugher. I stumbled out of bed to find the girls in a heap of gifts, tiaras on their heads.

"Santa came!" Susan yelled. The girls danced around excitedly. In that brief moment, I saw something new: hope.

CHAPTER 17

WHEN IAN ARRIVED LATER CHRISTMAS day, I gave him his gift. He loved it, but he smiled abashedly, admitting he'd pretty much forgotten it was Christmas.

Later, after we'd finished eating lunch and Ian was getting ready to head back into town, I asked him to check on Jamie. "He has the flu. He was looking pretty grim yesterday."

"You were by his place?" Ian asked. It was hard to miss the jealous tone in his voice.

I saw Frenchie's eyebrows rise, but she said nothing and continued to clear the dishes.

I nodded and handed Ian the sweater. "Don't forget your gift."

With a distracted smile, he stuffed it into his bag. "I'll be back tomorrow. We need to start planning the New Year's Eve party," he said. Unconsciously, he leaned in to kiss me. I turned my cheek.

Looking embarrassed, Ian gave me a light peck on the cheek then turned to leave.

"Be careful," I called as he stepped out onto the porch. He waved, jumped onto his snowmobile, and left, closing and locking the gate behind him.

I closed the front door, sliding the bars into place.

I turned to find Frenchie looking at me. She was grinning.

"Well, spit it out," I told her.

She shrugged. "You're using your head," she said with a grin and went into the kitchen.

Ian returned the next day with the news that Jamie was feeling better. I was relieved. We then got to work planning the New Year's Eve party. I was hyper-aware of the fact that Ian had plans and not just for the party. I would be his friend, I would forgive him for the past, but that was all there could be between us. Ian and I had nothing in common, no connection except our shared past. When I first arrived I thought I wasn't over him, but the more time I spent with him I realized I'd buried any real feelings long ago. I did not love him anymore. It seemed that Ian, on the other hand, thought the end of days had given him the chance to live a life almost missed. His misguided hope was becoming a problem.

"Hey, I have other news for you," Ian said.

I raised an eyebrow at him.

"Kiki and Gary finally had some luck with that radio."

"Really?"

"They picked up a signal and communicated for just a minute with someone."

"What do you mean?"

"Well, I guess someone asked where we were. They were able to give our location, but they couldn't get the signal to come back in again."

"At least we know we aren't the only ones still alive," I replied. "Maybe in the spring we can consider looking for other survivors."

Ian nodded.

In that same moment I noticed how tired he looked. Ian was not well and had started to look gaunt. Though he said he was fine, it was clear that he was having pain in his stomach. His meals became smaller and less frequent. When I tried to get him to eat more, he always said "leave it for the girls." I didn't buy it and as every day passed, I started to worry more.

Just after Christmas, Ian and I let the others know our idea about the party. At first people seemed resistant, but after a little convincing, the idea grew on them. Frenchie, Ian, and I, and a handful of others, spent two days reorganizing and decorating the elementary school gym. While Grandma's warning to be watchful was ever-present in my mind, the cold winter weather had ground the movement of the undead to a stop. With the exception of finding Clark in the Fletchers' field, it had been weeks since anyone had seen anything.

On New Year's Eve day, residents who could stand the cold weather were brought in by snowmobile or horse-drawn sled for the party. It turned out that the "decorative" Victorian era sled that had sat in the post office lobby longer than I could remember still worked. With a little reconfiguring, Fred Johnson had it running again. They'd managed to lasso in the Fletchers' horses, and Fred had become the town taxi driver.

"Looks beautiful," Summer gushed when she entered the gym. We'd found supplies from a recent prom that's theme had been something celestial. The entire place was decorated with silver crepe, stars, and moons. It was not overly done, just enough to make the event feel festive. Summer looked at least twenty pounds lighter. Her mother, who had always had dark-brown hair, had gone completely gray.

"I only had one bottle of dye left," she told me when she saw me looking at her hair. "I wanted to save it for when we are rescued," she explained with a laugh.

Rescued by whom, I wondered.

The others slowly trickled in. By the dinner hour there were thirty five of us. Harkening back to older and happier days, we shared food, eating at a long table in the middle of the room.

Jamie was one of the last to arrive. I heard his snowmobile buzz in. Moments later he entered, smiling, a large bag strapped to his back. I could tell he was up to something. I rose and fixed him a plate. He had just finished taking off his winter gear when I came up to him.

"This enough for you?" I asked, holding up the heaping plate of food.

He looked at it and me. "Who could ask for more?" He set the bag down and joined us at the table.

Ian was talking to Dusty and pushing his food from one side of the plate to another.

Jamie sat down and rubbed his hands together as he eyed over the plate. I slid into the seat beside him. He was about to dig in when he looked at his brother.

"Hey Ian, stop yapping and eat something," he said.

Surprised, Ian looked up. He said nothing, only nodded, and took a large bite of food. I turned to Jamie, wanting to share my worries about Ian's health, but something told me that he might not take my concern as intended.

"What did you make, Layla?" Jamie asked, turning back to his food.

I watched him eat a spoonful of beans. "The beans," I replied.

151

He stopped for a moment then chewed thoughtfully. "Hey, they are actually good."

Ethel, who'd been listening to the exchange, laughed.

Jamie looked inquisitively at her.

I smiled. "Ethel made those. I made the rice."

He looked down at his place. "I don't have any."

I laughed. "I know."

Several people around us chuckled, and I noticed then that no one had eaten the rice. Well, at least I had tried. I would remember, in the future, not to waste supplies with my weak attempts at cooking.

As the light began to wane, Tom and Mr. Jones disappeared. A few minutes later there was a strange humming sound. A backup generator kicked on. The emergency lights in the gymnasium cast a soft orange glow. Summer and several of the others lit candles Pastor Frank had brought with him. The room had a magical glow.

We had raided the liquor store and cases of champagne sat cooling outside. In the meantime, people were drinking wine and bottles of beer. Keeping Grandma's warning to be ever-watchful in mind, I didn't touch a drop. Others, however, did not hold back, and soon rowdy laughter filled the room.

Jamie, who'd also gone missing, finally reappeared with a cart on top of which he had something hidden under a sheet. Taking the cart to the end of the room, he pulled off the sheet to reveal an old gramophone. Jamie pulled out a record and put it on the player. He then wound the old machine. Dropping the needle, the gymnasium filled with the sound of 1920s big band music.

The stunned room fell silent. The music echoed.

The stir of mixed emotions in the room was palpable. Not sure what else to do, I went to Jamie and grabbed his hand. With a spin, he turned me onto the floor, and we broke out into dance.

The room fell into a clapping cheer and soon nearly everyone joined us.

"You're amazing," I told Jamie. "Where did you get that?"

"Don't you remember? It was in the library."

I smiled at him, and we moved across the floor grinning at one another. I felt like I was in a strange limbo in time. While I had refused to wear the yellow Big Bird dress, I did manage to shoplift a new, coffee-colored satin halter gown from Lil's shop.

Jamie smiled as he spun me, the cheerful gramophone music inspiring our steps. "You look beautiful, but I'm not sure if those accessories match," he said.

I had to laugh. While I wanted to look nice, I was also pragmatic so had worn my knee-high steel-toed winter boots, and my guns were holstered, my sword belted. "Never know when you'll need to kick ass," I said with a smile.

"So it seems Santa and his elves were at my house."

"Oh really?"

"I had this strange dream that an angel came in and took care of me. I woke to find my house clean, soup warming by the fire, and the heavenly smell of perfume in the air."

"Oh?"

"Yeah, I don't know what that perfume was, but it was amazing. I plan to buy stock in it."

"The stock market doesn't exist anymore."

"Ahh, that's right, I forgot," he said with a laugh. "I also found a very unique gift." He pulled out his hunting knife. On the leather strap tied to the hilt he'd strung the small pendant I'd left wrapped in the blue napkin. "Is this the one from the Fisherman's Wharf? The one the sea captain statue at the entryway was wearing on his hat? You remember, I asked the owner at the Wharf to sell it to me. That was right after I got back from Iraq."

"How should I know? Santa must have left it for you."

Just then the record stopped. Jamie paused to change records, rewinding the gramophone, and we started to dance again. This time the music was slow. The sweet gramophone music filled the space; I could hear everyone's happy, excited voices.

"Why did you like that pendant so much anyway?" I asked, taking the knife from him and looking at the pendant.

"One day, while my unit was out patrolling, I saw this symbol carved in stone on one of the buildings. I stopped to look at it. An old beggar was sitting there. He asked me if I knew what the symbol was. He told me it was called the flower of life and that it represents all life—us, the spirit world, everything—our interconnectedness. After that, I started seeing it everywhere. I couldn't believe my eyes when I saw it here, in Hamletville, at the Wharf. Santa was really nice to remember I liked it."

"Well, Santa is good at remembering important things."

A strong wind blew, causing the back door in the gymnasium to pop wide open. Everyone paused, and the two men on guard checked it out.

"Clear. Only the wind," Jensen called.

The happy mood returned at once. Almost everyone was dancing now, the lights in the room casting long shadows on the walls.

"I have something for you as well. It's a little late, but I wanted to give it to you myself."

Jamie handed me a small package wrapped in a cloth. From inside I pulled out a plastic squirt gun. It was filled with water. I was puzzled.

Jamie laughed at my expression. "There's holy water inside," he explained. "I stopped by the church and filled it."

I laughed out loud.

"I don't know why Grandma Petrovich wanted you to have holy water, but your grandma understood things better than anyone I ever knew. I figured I'd back her up on this one."

"Thank you," I said with a chuckle, putting my head against his chest, wrapping my arms around him.

I felt him stiffen a little, but then he relaxed, pulling me tight against him.

I closed my eyes and listened to the beating of his heart. It was all I wanted to hear.

When I opened my eyes again, I thought I saw a strange face in the crowd. Just for a moment, a thin, pale, and angry looking male face appeared amongst us. I pulled back to look more closely, but where I thought I had seen something, I now saw nothing. Shadows of dancing couples moved across the walls, but amongst the shadows I saw more figures than were actually in the room. Frantically, I looked around at the dancing couples but saw nothing unusual. All around me were the same faces I had seen over the last five months. Again, I looked at the shadows on the wall. Fast, shadowy images intermixed with those of the townspeople. I turned and saw another face, a female, who I did not know amongst the crowd. She was similar in appearance to the man. I strained to get a better look, but she disappeared. I stepped back from Jamie and pulled my gun from its holster.

"What is it?" Jamie whispered in alarm.

I looked around the room, a gun in one hand, the other on the hilt of my sword. A second later, the wind blew the door open again. At that same moment, the generator failed. The lights dimmed with a fading buzz leaving only candlelight. Cold wind gusted through the place, blowing out the candles nearest the door. I left Jamie's side. Grabbing a flashlight, I went to the doorway and flashed the light on the parking lot outside.

Overhead, the moon was full. It cast long shadows. The bare trees made claw-like images on the snowy ground. I pulled my coat off the wall and went outside, Jamie following fast behind me.

I snapped the flashlight off and pulled out my sword. I stood still, my eyes adjusting to the moonlight. I scanned the horizon. Nothing.

"What is it?" Jamie whispered.

I looked back. Several people stood in the gymnasium doorway looking out.

I said nothing but walked to the small slope at the side of the school. From there I could see much of the town and the frozen lake below. Jamie walked wordlessly beside me.

When I reached the slope, I scanned the vista. A second later, I saw it—them—something.

"There," I whispered to Jamie. I pointed my sword in the direction of the lake where strange, shadowy specters fled across the frozen ice. "Do you see that?" I asked him.

He was silent.

I watched the shadows retreat until I saw nothing more.

"Did you see that?" I asked him again, thinking maybe Grandma Petrovich's mushrooms had made me go half-crazy.

I looked up at Jamie. The startled look on his face told me he had seen it too.

"Layla—" he began.

"I know."

"What was it?" he asked.

I shook my head.

"What were they? What did you see?"

Indeed, what did I see? I was not exactly certain, but when I looked up at Jamie, one answer came clearly to mind: "Danger."

We stood wordlessly for a long time. Fear had frozen me in place.

Reassured by the lack of gunfire, happy sounds resumed inside the gym. A short while later, we heard the crowd counting down to midnight. Then there was a raucous cheer. It was a new year. They broke into a round of Auld Lang Syne. It shook me from the terror that had seized my throat.

I looked up at Jamie. He had a confused expression on his face.

I reached up and stroked his cheek. "I love you."

He looked as if I had startled him from dark thoughts. He paused a moment then leaned in and kissed me deeply. "I love you too," he whispered in my ear as he crushed me against him.

Together, we turned to go back to the gym.

Ian's shadowed figure was in the doorway.

Jamie paused.

Ian turned and walked back into the building.

"He'll accept . . . in time," I said.

Jamie didn't look so sure.

CHAPTER 18

FOR THE NEXT TWO MONTHS I watched for any sign of the shadowy figures I had seen on New Year's Eve. I never saw them again. I also did not see the forest lord and lady again though I had repeatedly gone looking for them.

Ian didn't come around anymore either. When I saw him in town, he paid me little attention. He was avoiding me. Jamie said he rarely came out unless he was on rotation. When Ian appeared in the school gym one day in March when he knew I would be there, I was surprised. I was even more surprised at his appearance. He was a shadow of his former self: his eyes were sunken, his clothes were hanging loose, and his cheeks were hollow.

"Jesus Christ, Ian, when was the last time you ate something," I asked as I crossed the room to join him. My stomach knotted.

A pained look crossed his face. I realized then he was having trouble standing. "Is Mrs. Finch here?"

I put my arm around his waist, steadying him, and led him to Mrs. Finch's office. "Come on, Ian, why didn't you say something? Just because things are complicated doesn't mean no one cares about you," I scolded.

Just as we reached Mrs. Finch, the fire alarm at the community center went off. We all stopped and counted: 1—2—3—4—5—6.

"Oh my god," Mrs. Finch whispered.

My heart leapt into my throat. "Stay here," I said as I lowered Ian into a chair. "I'll bar the door on my way out."

"Layla—" Ian began.

"We got it. Just stay here, and, for the love of god, let Mrs. Finch look you over. I'll come back," I said and tore down the hallway.

Frenchie and the girls stood, flabbergasted and afraid, in the middle of the gym. "Into Mrs. Finch's office and stay put," I told them but then paused. "Here," I said, taking the Magnum from the holster and pressing it into Frenchie's hands. "Aim for the head. Snap off the safety and fire," I said, showing her the gun. She nodded wordlessly and rushed her girls down the hallway.

Outside, I slammed the gymnasium door shut and dropped a bar over it.

I jumped on my bike and gunned it. The edges of the road were still covered in mounds of melting snow. While early spring vegetation was popping up, the weather was still cold and unpredictable.

I saw Will running toward the fire hall; he was carrying a rifle in each hand. I slowed, and he slid on behind me. Anyone who was armed had come running.

Jensen was in the middle of the community center parking lot looking frantic. "West barricade," he shouted at us. "There must be 50 of them!"

We set off at once. As we neared the west end of Main Street you could hear the sound of gunfire. The sight was horrifying. At least 50 undead were pressing against the street barricade. In some spots, they had nearly broken through. Some of the undead had started to trail down the barricade line, and soon they would find the weaknesses between the buildings.

Dusty and Fred were standing in the back of one pick-up. About five men stood in the back of another and were shooting into the oncoming horde.

"Holy shit," Will exclaimed.

When we pulled up, Will jumped off and climbed into the back of one of the trucks. I set off on the dirt bike to get to the undead trailing down the barricade lines.

I recognized the undead form of Brian Hoolihan. His farm was on the edge of town. He used to bring turnips to my grandmother. She would make soup out of them for him. He always liked my grandma; she was the only person he knew who like turnips or so he said. He lunged at the bike as I neared him. The barbed wire barricade kept us separated. With a heavy sigh, I shot him between his eyes.

Another undead, a young male who was moving quickly, neared a weakness in the line where the barricade passed the charred structure of the flower shop. I was amazed at how fast he moved. I spun the bike toward him, but it was slow in the soggy grass, grinding in the turf. I gave it some gas, and finally it lunged forward just as the young man bolted out of the ruins. He headed directly toward me.

I hit the gas to dodge him. When I did, the bike leapt forward but the snowy ground caused it to slide sideways. I found myself choosing between being caught and pulled to the ground by the bike or dealing with the undead youth bent on killing me. I jumped off. The bike fell sideways and slid across the mud. I tried to pull out the automatic, but it snagged on my winter jacket. In a heartbeat, the undead youth jumped at me.

My shashka, the scabbard strapped across my back, was out in a flash. I ducked and bolted sideways. I clambered onto a fence railing in the flower shop parking lot.

163

Having missed, the youth turned and lunged at me again. I jumped and as I turned sideways, slashed outward.

The blade connected. I kept myself upright, slid to a stop, then turned.

The youth had stopped. For a moment, he stood facing away from me. When he turned, I saw I had sliced off his hand. I stared at him; he stared back at me. Those milk-white eyes looked something other than dead. Was he thinking? Had he felt pain? Was he considering his next move?

He snarled, saliva and bloody foam dripping from his mouth, and lunged once more at me.

This time I faced him head on. I held my on-guard fencing stance and let him approach. Reel him in. Patience. Anticipate. He was quick, and his plan was simple: maul me. When he was within striking distance, I lunged. A split second later, he was hanging by his head from my sword, the shashka poking out of the back of his skull.

It took a moment for that strange light in his eyes to go out, and as I stared him down, a voice rasped inside my head. *Help us.*

My stomach shook. I couldn't tell if the voice had come from the people behind me or the boy hanging off the end of my sword.

"Layla!" Dusty screamed. They had broken through the barricade.

I shook the dead body loose. Taking a moment to rip off my jacket, I freed the automatic and ran back down the line to Main Street. Will and the others had climbed onto the roofs of the trucks and were shooting into the oncoming horde. Another truck pulled up; they shot out the window.

I eyed my options. At the back of Figgy's Old Vine Tavern was a stairwell leading to an upstairs apartment. It had a perfect line of fire on the street. I bolted up the steps and seconds later was raining bullets down on the oncoming horde. Careful to watch for civilians, I shelled the undead. Accuracy was a problem at this range, but their injured bodies fell and were more easily plucked off by the shooters below.

Moments later I heard a loud *BOOM*. My ears rung. A cloud of heavy smoke occluded the view for a moment; I then realized what had happened. Jeff was standing a few feet away from the old cannon that once sat outside of the VFW. The cannon had been parked in the center of the street just opposite the barricade. In front of the cannon, several undead lay on the ground, their bodies pierced with kitchen knives and other pieces of scrap metal. Jeff clambered away from the cannon and up onto one of the trucks.

I kept my eye on the barricade and blasted until the clip was empty. Like a complacent fool, I had not brought another.

I raised my gun, but if I shot, I could hit the living.

I pulled out the Glock and headed back down the stairs. Two of the undead who had spotted me met me at the bottom. They were easy marks.

I moved toward the dozen or so undead still straining at the townspeople. I jumped on top of a car and emptied the gun. It was not enough. The undead continued to make their assault.

Having left the Magnum with Frenchie, I was alone with my sword. I then saw Tom swinging axes in both hands and chopping his way through the undead horde. I bounded down and worked the other side of the crowd. Two arrows whooshed past my ear as Buddie Fowley appeared. Buddie had been found alive during the initial sweep. We all knew Buddie for his archery; he was the town's big game hunter. I turned to see the arrows hit their mark. With our Medieval weapons in hand, the three of us made the last stand for the town. We cut, slashed, and pierced our way through the remaining undead. The war was over shortly after; we had won the day.

Exhausted, I crawled into the back of one of the pickups and sat looking at the broken barricade. Main Street trailed off in the distance. The cannon pointed down the long road. A moment later, I heard a single gunshot. Jensen. I heard someone cry. I stared down the street beyond the broken barricade. Part of me was keeping an eye out for any stragglers. Another part of me was wondering about that voice I'd heard. I wanted to run, but I knew there was nowhere to go.

About ten minutes after it was over, two cars pulled up. I could hear Jamie's voice in the crowd. He found me a few minutes later.

"You okay?" he asked.

I didn't know how to answer.

He stepped in front of me, blocking my vision of the road. It broke the trance. "Layla," he whispered, tipping my chin up toward him. "You okay?" he asked again.

"Yeah, it is what it is, right?" I replied, kissing his hand. I slid the sword back into the scabbard then climbed onto the roof of the truck. People were sitting around looking hopeless.

I whistled sharply, getting everyone's attention. "Town meeting in two hours. Between now and then we need to get this barricade refortified and these bodies moved. Who can help?" I asked.

There was a silence for a moment then a flood of volunteers. Within five minutes the arrangements had been made and everyone went to work.

I bounced off the truck and grabbed Jamie by the hand. "Ditched the bike. Wanna help me see if she still runs? We need to head back to the school."

"Why?" he asked as we walked toward my bike.

"I left Frenchie there," I replied, not wanting to get into Ian's issue yet.

As we passed the body of the boy I had killed, Jamie stopped. "Hey, that was the Klein's son. He was some kind of piano virtuoso. I guess they used to homeschool him so he could spend time practicing the piano. He played at the church sometimes. Nice kid."

Guilt wracked me as I looked down on him. He *had* tried to kill me. I wondered then—why? Why were they trying to kill us? Consume us? I then realized that the boy looked practically intact save a nasty scratch across his still-fleshy, though pale and somewhat saggy, chest.

"Hey, didn't you say they should just be bones by now?" I asked Jamie.

He shrugged. "Guess I was wrong," he said as he picked the bike up. "Looks like you just broke a mirror." He climbed on the bike and started it. "All good. I get to drive this time," he said, and we headed off.

I could not help but look back at the boy's body once more and think of how he had paused when I'd taken his hand. The implications made me shudder.

CHAPTER 19

"CANCER," MRS. FINCH WHISPERED TO Jamie and me.

Ian sat looking at the floor, his chin propped in the palm of his hand.

"Are you sure?" Jamie asked aghast.

I stared at Ian.

"There is only so much I can tell. I did a quick blood and urine analysis and a physical. From the symptoms described, test results, and the condition he is in, it is most likely cancer. I can't even say for sure what kind, but based on his pain, could be liver, stomach, or pancreas. I just don't know."

Jamie went silent, and Ian still had not looked up.

"What about treatment?" I asked.

Mrs. Finch shook her head. "Chemo and that sort of thing are just not feasible. There might be some meds in the pharmacy, but we're shooting in the dark without a proper physician."

"And what if you're wrong?" I asked.

"Layla," Jamie said with a frown.

Ian looked up. "She's right, Layla."

"So we do nothing? We just wait for him to get sicker and—"

"—and die" Ian finished.

Frenchie tapped the glass of the office window. The alarm on the community center had rung more than two hours past. By now, everyone was waiting, and it was already dark. Nerves were running high. I waved to her that we were coming.

"Let's go," Ian said and rose.

Jamie took him gently by the arm, but Ian shrugged his brother off. "I'm good," was all he said.

In the gym, Ian sat at the back while the rest of us went to the front.

I sat down on the stage.

"The barricade is back in place. Tomorrow we're going to kick on enough juice to weld. We bulldozed steel and scrap in and will do more tomorrow. For tonight, it is good enough," Tom informed the crowd.

As he spoke, I thought about how much fuel was left. Reserves were getting low.

"What happened today? Who were those people?" Ethel asked.

"Mostly farm folks," Fred Johnson replied.

"All at once?" Ethel asked.

It was a question that had been burning in everyone's mind.

"Looks like pack mentality," Buddie added.

"Mentality? Like they are thinking?" Summer asked.

"Something like that, you know, like animals . . . maybe," Buddie answered.

"There could be more attacks like this. There are at least four dozen more farms and vineyards out there, and those are just the ones near us," Mr. Jones added.

"Well, we lived, didn't we," Jeff commented.

"Barely," Dusty added, "and we lost Jensen."

The room was silent. Suddenly I saw Will and Kiki who had been keeping watch by the door stiffen and pull their weapons.

"Movement," Will called.

A dozen armed citizens raced across the room, but something in me froze. My whole body felt stiff. Jamie headed toward the door, turning to look inquisitively at me as to why I had not followed. I neither moved nor said a word. Confused, he went ahead. My hands shook. My ears were ringing, and the strange feeling of electricity filled the air.

At the door, people were talking and moments later the crowd broke into smiles. They then ushered two strangers into the room: two unfamiliar men soon stood in the center of a circle of the townspeople.

I watched them from afar. I knew without a doubt that something about them was not right.

They smiled in a very pleasing manner, but it was a false smile. Physically, they were both very attractive. One was tall, muscular, and had shoulder length sandy-colored hair. The second was shorter and darker in complexion. His head was shaved, and he had heavy eyebrows and a hawkish expression. They were both dressed rather oddly. Their dark clothing looked too tight, buttons closed too close to the neck, and the fashion seemed outdated. My hands trembled.

Jamie was standing a bit back from the crowd, but I could see from the expression on his face that he was not sold either. Regardless, Tom led the men to the front of the room. Everyone had risen from their seats to get a closer look.

"Layla, these men have come to speak to us," Tom said excitedly. Tom's jubilant nature overcame him, and he didn't wait for my reaction but pressed the two men forward.

They paused and looked at me, but I said nothing. I slid off the stage.

The two men looked around the room. I noticed the tall one pause when he saw Kira and Susan. He stared at them as the other began to speak.

"My name is Corbin," the shaven one began.

I stepped between the girls and the fair-haired man's gaze and pulled the shashka from its scabbard.

Startled, the stranger looked at me. His eyes were icy blue. He tried to feign a smile.

I lifted the sword and set it on my shoulder.

He looked away.

"This is Finn," Corbin said, referring to the fair one. I noticed that Corbin's eyes were also ice blue. "We have just arrived by boat. As you know, the lake has thawed, and we are going around looking for survivors."

"Where are you based?" Pastor Frank asked.

Corbin looked the pastor over in great detail before he answered. There was something odd in Corbin's movements, a sort of strange control. "There is a very large group of us on Enita Island at the HarpWind Grand Hotel. The island is isolated. The disease never came there. We have been able to keep the hotel running using much of its Victorian era equipment. We're trying to collect as many survivors there as possible."

"Why?" Jamie asked.

Enita Island was famed for its seclusion and opulent Grand Hotel. I'd once seen a documentary about it but had never been there myself. Unreachable by land, one had to take a ferry to get to the hotel. The story was plausible. The storytellers were not.

Corbin considered Jamie. "There is survival in numbers. We are armed and have considerable supplies. We also have three doctors."

I looked back at Ian who was still sitting. He'd heard.

"The island is completely sheltered. These creatures cannot reach us. It is a place of safety, a place to begin again. Our goal is to find people to join us," Corbin added.

"What about help from the outside, the government?" Kiki asked.

Corbin shrugged. "There is no government. Everything has fallen."

"How did you find us?" I asked them.

They both turned and looked at me and then exchanged a glance between them. In that moment, I heard a strange murmuring sound in my head.

"We were cruising the shoreline and heard the sound of gunfire. Was there an incident?" Corbin asked.

"Yeah, man, but we whooped ass," Jeff replied.

Corbin smiled at Jeff as one might smile at a small, stupid pet. "We can keep you safe from such onslaughts. Last I knew, these creatures cannot swim."

Several people laughed.

Ian had risen and was standing at the back of the crowd. He was listening intently as the townspeople began shooting a barrage of questions at the strangers: how many people were already there, kinds of supplies, space available, plan for the future, etc., etc. Corbin and Finn had ready answers, too many ready answers. And all of the answers they had were good ones. In that moment, I remembered something my grandma used to say: "I ran from the wolf only to run into the bear." Whatever they were selling, I wasn't buying.

The questioning went on for what seemed like an eternity. They had heard nothing from the outside either. They were gathering what survivors they could. They already had more than 100 people at the hotel. They heard the cities were overrun. They had no idea what caused it. We weren't safe where we were. They wanted to hit the reset button on civilization, starting over on their island.

Ethel invited the strangers to stay the night and eat with us, but they insisted they return to their boat. They promised to return the next day and asked us to be ready to go. Everyone was in an excited jitter. That night, people left the gymnasium full of dreams. Who wouldn't have?

Back at the cabin, the girls crowded around their mother in the kitchen.

"Will all three of us stay together in one room at the hotel?" Kira asked.

"I want the hotel!" Susan yelled happily.

"I think so," Frenchie told them.

"Do you think there will be other kids there?" Kira quizzed her mother.

"Probably," Frenchie told them absently as she set their dinner down in front of them.

I was standing in the doorway of the kitchen listening to the exchange. Frenchie looked up at me. Apparently I was not doing a good job hiding my concerns.

"What is it?" she asked.

"Don't go with them," I said.

Frenchie set down the jar of peanut butter. The girls stopped their chatter and looked at me.

"Why not?"

It was a question I didn't know how to answer. "It's not safe," I replied.

"Well, if we get another influx like the one today, we're not safe here either," she replied.

I shook my head.

"What is it?"

"Just don't go. I can't say why. It's instinct, I guess. But I know it's not safe, especially for the girls."

Frenchie looked thoughtfully at me. "Like a Grandma Petrovich instinct?"

I nodded.

Frenchie frowned, causing lines to cross her forehead.

"Mom," Kira called in a sing-song, knowing her dream of living in the hotel was fast fading.

"I'll think about it," was all Frenchie said in reply, answering both of us.

CHAPTER 20

ON THE FIRST DAY OF spring every year, my grandmother would go into the woods and return with a basket full of forsythia and daffodils. When I woke at first light the next day, I lay in bed considering the weight of obligations on me. I also worried about the new burden I must bear: stopping the exodus. The stress of everything overwhelmed me. How could I convince everyone to stay in Hamletville based solely my hunch that there was something wrong with these people? Instead of doing what I should do, I slid on my boots and headed over the back gate into the woods in search of forsythia and daffodils.

I hiked into the woods and followed Spring Creek, one of the many small tributaries that ran to the lake, deeper into the forest. The soft sounds of the water trickling over the rocks soothed my mind and let me think more clearly. There was still ice at the creek's edges. Growing in small clumps on the creek bank, I saw snow drops and the first spring daffodils. There was a clean smell in the air. I'd been hiking for about an hour when I stopped to rest on a fallen log. Mushrooms grew from the wood's decayed crevices. I looked around and noticed that fresh spring ferns were growing in abundance, their curled fingers unfolding in the morning light which cast slanted beams as it broke through the trees. Bright green moss covered the rocks on the forest floor.

I sat still, looking at the water, when I heard rustling behind me.

I turned to find a small girl standing there. She was standing in a small grassy space between a dense part of the woods and me. She was the most beautiful child I'd ever seen. Her hair was as yellow as an August sunflower. It curled wildly around her ears. She wore a green cotton tunic with a pale green top underneath and earth-colored pants. She was about Kira's age. When she saw me, she smiled. She skipped over the grass toward me.

As she came closer, my skin turned to goose-bumps.

She climbed on the log beside me, adjusting back and forth until she found a comfortable nook. I noticed she had a sort of diadem on her head: a sparkling freshwater pearl glittered on her forehead. Her eyes glittered similarly; they were the same chartreuse green of the new ferns. And I also noticed that her ears were somewhat pixie looking in shape, and the skin around the edge of her hairline was tinged green.

She whistled a sweet sound into the forest. A moment later, a spring fawn appeared. Its wide nostrils breathed deeply, smelling both the girl and me.

The girl dangled her feet as she dug in her pocket. She pulled out what looked like lumps of raw sugar. She held out her hand to the fawn. Hesitantly, the dappled creature stepped forward, keeping one watchful eye on me. After a moment, it was licking the sweet morsel from the girl's hand. She giggled.

She handed one of the sugary treats to me. I extended my hand to the fawn. It considered for a moment then took the treat from me as well.

The girl giggled again.

After the fawn had eaten our treats, it trotted back into the forest.

The girl smiled at me and slid off the log. She skipped back toward the dense woody area from which she came. At the border between the small open space and the thick forest stood the magisterial forest lady I had seen that winter. She wore a pale yellow gown.

The woman motioned to the child. The girl wrapped her arms around the woman's legs. The tall lady, holding her hair back, bent and kissed the child on the head. Then she rose and motioned for me to follow.

She took the child by the hand, and they turned toward the woods.

I was not afraid, but I was uncertain.

She stopped. Seeing I was not coming, she bent low and whispered in the child's ear. The girl nodded and ran back to me. She stood in front of me and extended her hand much the same way she'd extended it to the fawn. She smiled sweetly.

I took the child's hand. It was surprisingly warm.

The sweet creature smiled up at me, and we trailed behind the tall woman. We crossed the grass and moved into the dense woods. The child led me over rocks and fallen logs. After a few moments, we reached a clearing. The tall woman was sitting at an old well. It was stone at its base and had a pitched wooden roof covering it. A short distance away was a dilapidated old cottage. I had never noticed it before, but I knew there were old houses deep in the forest.

The child let go of my hand and ran to the woman.

The woman smiled at me. "Are you afraid?" she asked. Her voice was light and sweet like the sound of a songbird.

I had wondered if they would ever talk. "No," I replied.

She smiled. "Vasilisa was not afraid either."

Vasilisa was my grandmother's given name. "My grandmother feared little."

"The old blood, the wise blood, that ran in her veins showed her right from wrong, good from evil. It helped her see."

Again, my grandmother's words. "And what should I see?" I asked the woman.

She looked thoughtfully at me. "Why ask me? You already know. The old blood is in you as well."

"The men who came are not human."

"Not anymore," the woman answered.

"And they are a threat."

"Yes."

"What should I do?"

"Stop them from leaving."

"And if I cannot?"

She looked down into the well and motioned for me to join her.

I came to the well and looked inside. At first I saw only my reflection in the spring sunlight. After a moment, however, the image swirled, and I saw myself talking to the townspeople who looked back at me with frowning faces. Shadows appeared amongst them, whispering in their ears. The image swirled again, and I saw a massive boat docked at the end of the community pier. Everyone was walking toward it. Moonlight bounced on the water then dark clouds covered the moon and everything went black. The image disappeared.

"You must protect them," she told me.

I looked at the woman. The girl had moved off in the distance and was picking flowers. The doe-eyed lady whose skin was also tinged green at the edges smiled sympathetically at me.

"Who are you?" I asked.

"Vasilisa called us Leshi, forest spirits. Many years ago, a girl named Berwyn lived in that house. She called us Aes Sídhe. The old ones of this land, they have also come to you, called us Pukwudgie."

"Why do the forest spirits care what happens to us? To me?"

She set her hand on mine. "Mankind has finally consumed itself. Can any spark of humanity survive? You must go now. And you must try. Much depends on you."

I rose and turned to go back. Before I left, I looked at her once more. "What is your name?"

Her facial features softened. "Peryn."

I nodded and headed back out of the woods.

"Farewell and be blessed, Layla," she called.

When I looked back again, they were both gone.

CHAPTER 21

WHEN I GOT TO THE cabin, Frenchie and the girls were not there.

I slid on the bike and headed for the school. When I got there, I found the townspeople packing the supplies.

"What are you doing?" I demanded loudly when I entered.

They stopped. Everyone looked confused. "We're getting ready," Summer replied.

Frenchie didn't look at me.

"Who says we are going? We haven't even discussed it."

Tom set a box down. "We didn't know there was anything to discuss."

Ian and Jamie emerged from the back.

"Well, there is. We can't go with those people," I said.

Everyone looked surprised.

"Why not?" Mrs. Finch asked.

"It's not safe. Didn't you all see it? They aren't right. They aren't normal. We can't believe their story. They want something from us."

Jamie looked worried.

"But it's a chance at a fresh start," Pastor Frank said.

"Didn't you notice it, Pastor? Didn't you see it? You're a man of God, after all."

"See what?"

I shook my head. "I'm telling you all, those people are dangerous."

Everyone looked blindsided.

"You're just being paranoid," Jeff informed me.

"We need to do something. We can't just sit here and wait to get attacked again. We're never going to make it," Mr. Jones said.

"We made it all winter," I retorted.

"It's not just that. Here we are just surviving. We need to move on," Tom told me.

"Well, I, for one, am going," Jeff said. "No offense, but it's pretty much a sausage fest around here."

I rolled my eyes. "Please listen to me," I pleaded and cast a glance at Jamie and Ian for help. "Please, I'm telling you. Those people are not what they seem. Don't you think they had too many good answers? Too many ready and easy explanations? They are dangerous."

"Why do you think that?" Jamie asked.

The room was still. It was time to play the only card I had left. "Everyone knows what Grandma Petrovich was. I am telling you, I *know* just like Grandma *knew* things. And those people are dangerous."

I had silenced the room.

After a few minutes passed, Pastor Frank spoke: "Many respected your grandmother, Layla, but we need to try."

I looked at everyone.

"You all agree?" I asked.

While some nodded, others looked away, not wanting to make eye contact with me.

I walked to the door. "Then go without me," I yelled, slamming the door behind me.

I had just slid onto my bike when Jamie came out and stopped me.

"I think you're right," he said. "I sensed it too."

"Good, then maybe you can convince them."

He shook his head. "It's no use. Their minds are made up. Hell, they never even considered not going until you said something. Those men painted a good picture."

"Well, we can stock up at the cabin. If we stay alert, we'll be fine. Even if anything gets through, the chances of them finding the cabin are slim."

Jamie took a deep breath and looked away from me.

"What?"

"Ian is going to go. There are doctors there."

I stared at him. "And?"

"And I need to go with him."

I kick-started the bike. "Well, good! I guess the two of you can die together then," I said and gunned it. Before Jamie could say another word, I was gone.

I spent the rest of the day in the barn mulling over my own survival. Would I be able to make it on my own? I sat with a whet stone sharpening my swords, reorganizing my ammo, and trying to think about hunting. What I was really thinking about, however, was how I had failed everyone. My grandmother lay buried behind the barn. Ian was dying. The woman in the forest charged me with protecting my people—and she was not the first to do so—but I had failed to convince anyone. I had even failed to make the man who loved me stay. I had failed my grandmother with my inability to see. I had failed in my ability to convince anyone of anything. As a result, I would be alone. And they would be dead.

Later that afternoon, Frenchie came by to grab her belongings. She was planning to take the girls to Summer's and Ethel's so she would be closer to town when the visitors returned.

"I do believe you," she told me as she left. The girls crowded beside their mother.

"Then why are you going?" I asked.

She stood on the porch, bags in hand. "Because neither your instinct nor this life are enough," she replied and stepped off the porch toward Will's truck. "I'm sorry," she added.

"Your daughters are alive because of instinct," I called after her.

She stopped.

"Your instinct," I added. "And what does your instinct—not your mind—tell you?"

She frowned heavily and loaded her girls into the truck; they drove away.

I stomped back into the cabin and threw my gear on the couch. I sat down at the kitchen table and put my head in my hands. After a few minutes, I heard the kitchen chair across from mine slide across the floor. I looked up to see my grandmother sitting there.

Tu-tu-tu-tu-tu, she clicked at me.

I realized then that I'd been crying. I wiped my eyes and looked at my grandmother.

That boy. He loves you, and you love him. You'll send him off to die like that? Come now, that is not my Layla, she said.

"What can I do? They won't listen to me."

What did Peryn say?

"To stop them."

Ah-hum, my grandma considered, her ghostly fingers tapping on the table. They made no sound. *Are you sure?*

I thought back. "Well, I guess what she said was I should protect them."

My grandma tapped her finger on her nose then pointed at me. *You can't hide an axe in a sack. When the truth outs, who will be there for them if you are not?*

I lowered my head. She was right.

My grandmother rose. *Layla, I like that boy. You know, he bandaged my toe once when I tripped at the grocery store.*

Suddenly, I felt ashamed.

No, no, my grandma said as she exited the kitchen. *Enough sulking. Get to work. And Layla?* she called from the living room.

"Yes, Grandma?"

Don't forget the holy water.

"Grandma?" I called.

She did not answer.

I rose and followed her to the living room. She was gone.

Through the cracks in the window slats, I saw movement in the driveway outside. I peeked through; one of the undead was standing in the there. I realized then that I had been so annoyed with Frenchie that I'd forgotten to close the gate.

Picking up my sword, I opened the door. The creature, a man, turned and looked when he heard me.

He did not rush me as many of the others had but simply stood, his head cocked to the side, observing me.

My eyes darted around. He appeared to be the only one who had gotten in, but I would have to check to be sure. I suddenly felt afraid. What if there were more? What if I overlooked something? I could die, alone, in this moment, and no one would know. And I had not even told Jamie I was sorry.

"Why don't you just go away," I told the undead man.

He pulled himself upright, arching his back, then turned and slowly shuffled out of the driveway back down Fox Hollow Road. I watched him go, keeping an eye out for any others. After he left, I barred the gate and did a complete sweep of the property. I found nothing, no one, alive or dead.

I sat down on the porch steps, sword in hand, and closed my eyes. What had I become? What was this new world where I saw strange things at every turn? Forest spirits. Shadows. Was I hearing the undead? Were they hearing me? I fully realized then that there was no going back. Whatever I was, whatever I had become, there was no return. I had to embrace it or run from it. If I ran, people I loved, people for whom I was responsible, might die.

When I opened my eyes, I noticed the sun had set. I rose. After making a stop at the barn for supplies, I went inside and packed up my gear. I closed all the shutters and padlocked all the doors from the outside. I then hopped on my bike. Chaining the gate closed, I headed away from Fox Hollow Road.

As I sped down the drive, I found the undead man lumbering along. I pulled out my gun but did not shoot. He stopped when I passed but didn't lunge at me.

I gunned the bike and headed to town, hoping Jamie would forgive my hasty words, hoping I was not too late. And I remembered to bring the holy water.

CHAPTER 22

IT WAS DARK BY THE time I pulled into Jamie's house. Though there was no wind, the leaves on the Birch trees outside had turned over and were shaking. Odd. Grandma always said the leaves would turn when a storm was coming. I looked up at the moon. No clouds. No wind.

The house was dark. I knocked heavily. There was no answer.

"Jamie?" I called.

Nothing.

I went to the window and peeked inside. It was totally dark; there was no movement.

He must have gone to Ian's house. I jumped back on the bike and headed across town. There was no sign of anyone anywhere. Neither the dead nor the living stirred.

Ian's and Kristie's house sat on upper Seneca Street. Kristie's grandmother had left the house to them when she died. It was a large, white, two-story Colonial with an attached greenhouse. The greenhouse had fallen into disrepair, weeds growing wildly inside. The house was empty.

I was about to head toward the elementary school when I heard a horn blast from the lake. I pulled out my binoculars. From Ian's porch, I had a good view. What looked like the last of the town residents were filing down the dock and being loaded aboard the ship. Almost everyone was on board already. Mrs. Finch was pushing Ian in a wheelchair down the dock toward the boat. I could see Jamie at the ship's plank arguing with the man who had introduced himself as Corbin. The last few residents were just boarding.

"Oh my god," I whispered. I would be left behind.

I jumped on the bike and gunned it. Praying someone would see my headlight, I sped across town, cutting through lawns and the grocery store parking lot. As I blasted through, I noticed several undead had collected just outside the town library. They paused, watching as I passed. I swerved by them and headed toward the water. Down over the bank, passing the Fisherman's Wharf, I hit the lakeside walking path. I sped toward the boat.

I noticed that two men were pulling up the plank. Jamie was there with them, talking incessantly, waving his arms. Tom pulled him out of the crewman's way.

Then, they heard the bike. I saw Jamie shout to the men and point toward me. The men paused.

I drove the bike down the dock and parked it under the pavilion. Jumping off, I jogged down the wooden planks, hopping the swinging pedestrian gate, and ran to the end.

Corbin, the hawkish looking man, stood at the rail. The crewman seemed to wait for his command. He looked down at me. When our eyes met, I could feel him challenging me.

"Sorry I'm late," I said with a smile, trying to play it off.

He wasn't buying me anymore than I was buying him.

"Let her on," I heard Jamie yell, but I could not see him.

Corbin leaned over the railing to look more closely at me. We were standing nearly face to face. "Should I let you on?" he whispered.

I held his gaze, not backing down. "Let me on."

He motioned to the men to lower the plank.

I looked at him.

This time, he smiled at me. "Remember later, *you* asked to come," he whispered.

"I'm here to keep those I love safe. *You* remember that," I replied, holding his gaze.

He smiled, motioned for me to come aboard, then he disappeared back into the ship.

The steel rail felt cold beneath my hand. I turned and looked back toward the town. There, above the town on the Point, I saw the figure of a man. He leaned back into an archer's pose. He shot a shadow arrow that burned like a shooting star across the night's sky. I took a deep breath and boarded the ship.

CHAPTER 23

I WAS MET ON BOARD BY the smiles of the people I had come to love.

Jamie fought his way through the crowd and grabbed me, nearly crushing me. "You're pressing my throwing daggers into my back," I whispered to him.

He let go with a chuckle and looked down at me.

"I'm sorry," I said rapidly, the words falling too loudly and somewhat broken from my mouth.

"No, no, it's okay. I'm sorry too. I understand," he said, kissing the top of my head.

I pressed my cheek against his chest. I opened my eyes to see Ian looking at us. He looked away.

"Why did you change your mind?" Jamie asked. He took my hand and led me toward the railing. The boat had turned and was now gliding across the lake. The town was no longer in sight.

"Well, I needed a vacation. I hear the HarpWind is nice."

Jamie smiled wryly. "Seriously," he whispered.

I turned and looked back toward the Captain's deck of the yacht. Therein I could see the heads of our new benefactors. "I'm not wrong, and I haven't changed my mind," I said.

He looked at them as well. "Yeah, well, we'll see, won't we?"

It took about three hours to cross the lake in the swift yacht. Soon, the lights of the HarpWind Grand Hotel appeared on the horizon. The place was dimly lit; they were using candles and lanterns. The hotel's lights appeared like ghostly shadows on the water, breaking amongst the waves.

The captain of the boat sounded the horn.

It was met by the clang of a cast-iron triangle at the end of the hotel's pier.

Jamie and I exchanged glances.

When we arrived, a number of people were there to greet us. Many were other survivors who shook our hands and asked us from where we'd come. They were a mixed group coming from small towns and cities scattered all around the Great Lakes. Amongst them were hotel proprietors who helped us make our way up the path to the opulent HarpWind Grand Hotel.

"I need to help Ian," Jamie whispered to me.

I nodded and then, dodging through the crowd, I found Frenchie. I picked up Susan and set her onto my shoulders. She laughed. "It's beautiful," she said, looking at the hotel.

She was right. It was beautiful. The hotel was five stories in height and stretched long. It curved with the shape of the land, making the hotel crescent shaped. I remembered that the word Enita, the name of the island, meant moon; I'd see it in the documentary. The first two floors of the hotel were stone; the upper floors were New England style shingle sided. As we walked toward the massive structure, I could see the chandelier in the foyer was alive with candlelight. The crystals sparkled.

Frenchie took my hand. "Thank you," she whispered.

We were led into the main foyer. A massive stone fireplace burned cheerfully. It stemmed off the cool chill in the air.

A pale looking girl with long black hair and flashing pale blue eyes introduced herself as Matilda. She began handing out room keys and taking names. The more I looked at her, the more I realized I recognized her as the face I had seen amongst the crowd on New Year's Eve. When she got to me and Frenchie, she paused. She looked thoughtfully at me. I looked back with a hard gaze.

"That man said that you, the girl with the sword," she said, looking at the weapon hanging from my belt, "are roomed with him: 415," she said, smiling sweetly as she handed me a key.

I took the key but shot Jamie an inquisitive look. He smiled bashfully and shrugged.

"And you are?" she said, looking at Frenchie.

"Frenchie Davis, and this is Kira and Susan," she introduced, but I squeezed Frenchie's hand hard, and she said no more.

"Aw, how cute," Matilda said, looking at Kira and Susan. The expression on her face told me she thought they were anything but cute.

"She needs a room beside mine," I told Matilda.

Matilda turned to look at me, and I noticed that same odd movement about her I had seen in Corbin. She stared at me for a moment. "I'm sorry, I have nothing available, but I do have 313 for you, Ms. Davis. There are two beds in that room," she replied and handed Frenchie a key.

After she'd gone, I joined Jamie and Ian. Jamie was standing at the back of Ian's wheelchair.

"Where are you?" I asked Ian. He was holding a key in his hand.

"They put me on the ground floor near the infirmary: room 195. I guess the doctor will be able to see me right away. I'm going now," Ian said.

I took Jamie's bag from his shoulder. "I got this."

Jamie nodded. "I'll be up in a few."

Ian looked away, but I had seen the look on his face.

Jamie turned and pushed Ian down the hallway.

Matilda had finished passing out the keys and was standing with the clipboard at the check-in table. I noticed another man behind the counter. He had the same odd way about him as the others and had long, black hair, light eyes, and pale skin.

I went up to them. Trying to play nice, I smiled at Matilda. "I'd like a copy of that list," I said, looking down at her clipboard.

She looked surprised. "Whatever for?"

As I looked at her, I thought about how easily we fall for anyone who seems to be in authority. Our natural paranoia, eroded by near bombardment of our private lives, had stripped us of the instinct to shelter ourselves from strangers. Everyone I loved had put their name on that list. I gave Matilda a hard look.

In that moment, I saw a dark shadow pass over her face, the mask falling away. She covered it quickly. "Well, as you know, we have no Xerox," she said with a smile. "Perhaps Ambrosio will write the list down for you?" she said, looking to the man.

He looked me over from head to foot. "You may stop by for it tomorrow."

I knew there would never be a list if I depended on them. "Don't trouble yourself," I said, taking the clipboard from her hand. "I got it."

She looked astonished and gazed at the man she'd called Ambrosio.

I grabbed a sheet of paper off the counter and jotted down the room numbers of the Hamletville citizens.

"We didn't get your name," Ambrosio told me, coming around from behind the counter to stand in front of me.

I smiled, handed Matilda her clipboard, and set the pen down. "No, you didn't," I said and walked away.

As I left, I heard them murmuring between one another.

I was there, but I didn't have to like it.

CHAPTER 24

IT TURNED OUT THAT ROOM 415 was a bridal suite; there was a plaque on the door. I set down the bags and looked the space over. It was beautiful. Someone had lit a number of candles, filling the space with a soft, romantic glow. A large poster bed was draped with gauzy white cloth. The bed was covered in a light purple satin coverlet. The ornate Victorian furniture was romantic. A settee piled with pillows looked out at the lake. The moonlight was reflecting on the pitching waves.

For a moment, I pretended. I pretended the world had not fallen apart. I pretended that the undead were not walking around. I pretended that earth spirits were not talking to me. I pretended I'd come home from D.C. on vacation and had fallen in love with Jamie. I pretended we had gotten married and that my grandmother had smiled benevolently on me, me dressed in white, as Jamie and I married in a Russian Orthodox ceremony. I pretended that Jamie had brought me here as a honeymoon surprise. I played pretend, just for a moment, and then I was done. It did not do to play pretend.

I went to the window and checked the lock. It was bolted loosely from the inside. I removed the ornate tiebacks from the window and laced them around the window locks. I then checked the room for any other entrances. The only other way to get in was the front door. I dragged the writing desk from one side of the room and jammed the door handle, barricading the door.

I pulled the curtains shut then unrolled my weapons bundle. I stood looking down on them, considering what to do next. I checked the cartridge on the Glock and stuffed it into the holster. I reloaded the Magnum and did the same. There was a small ammo pouch on the holster; inside, I stuffed the holy water inside—just in case. I also stuffed Jamie's water gun, still loaded, into a pocket. I adjusted the shashka scabbard to bandolier style and threaded the throwing daggers onto a belt. From my boots I pulled out the doe and wolf poyasni. I slid each across the small whet stone I carried in the weapon roll then stuffed them back into my boots.

A short while later there was a knock on the door.

I leaned against the door, sword drawn, and looked through the keyhole.

"Layla?" Jamie called.

I moved the desk and opened the door.

"I would have just come in, but I didn't want you to shoot me."

"I had the door barricaded anyway," I said, motioning to the desk.

He laughed. "I heard." He then looked around the room, at least the parts of it I had not dismantled. "Wow. This is really something."

"Well, it is the bridal suite."

Jamie look embarrassed. "Look, I'm not trying to, you know, force any issue. I just wanted you safe—with me. That's all."

I laid my sword on the bed and wrapped my hands around his neck. I pulled him into a deep kiss, my hand sliding across his back and shoulders, fingers toying with the hair at the base of his neck. He held me tightly, pressing my body against him. I could feel the heat rising between us.

Again, there was a knock on the door.

We broke apart, both of us breathing heavily.

Jamie regained his composure and answered the door. I picked up the shashka.

"All right," he said to whoever was on the other side, "okay, thank you," he added and then closed the door. "We're invited for a nightcap in an hour. The hosts want to welcome us," he said.

"The hosts, eh?" I looked back at my weapons. "How is Ian?"

"They got him settled in and the doctor was by to take some blood. He said they are going to do as many tests as they can. Mrs. Finch was by and told them what she'd already seen. Ian was really tired and wanted to sleep so I left him be."

"What about the doctor? How did he seem?"

"Normal. He is from a research hospital in Ohio."

"I don't like leaving Ian alone," I said.

"Me either. This whole thing is—I don't know what it is. I mean, I saw those shadows too."

"There are other strange things out there as well; I've seen spirits, earth spirits, ancestral spirits, I don't know what, exactly."

Jamie raised his eyebrows at me in surprise.

"I think my grandma was right. She always said that we are not alone in this world. We humans, we are not the only creatures on this plane. Now than humankind is not creating so much noise, maybe those other things in this world are more apparent."

Jamie looked thoughtful. "And what the hell are these people?"

I pulled out the squirt gun Jamie had given me. It had seemed a funny gift at the time. We both looked at it.

"The holy water," Jamie said considering.

I nodded.

Jamie took the little yellow and blue plastic gun and looked at it; his forehead furrowed.

"What are you thinking?" I asked.

"Well, Grandma Petrovich got all those guns and everything, right? You used all that stuff to protect us. And she also got holy water."

I waited.

"Well, it's obvious, isn't it? Every movie, T.V. show, comic book, video game—there is only one thing that you can kill with holy water," Jamie said.

And in the moment, it was obvious.

"Vampires?" I whispered.

He nodded.

"But these people seem like . . . I don't know what. They aren't like the classic or romantic stories you hear. There is something awkward about them. Do you know what I mean? I'm not afraid, I just . . . "

" . . . just don't want to deal with their shit? Well, we've spent the last half year being chased by the undead. Maybe it has numbed us."

I shrugged. "What is this world we're living in?"

"And what do they want from us?" Jamie replied.

Indeed, what did they want?

205

CHAPTER 25

"BLOODY HELL," JEFF EXCLAIMED AS we stood in front of more food than any of us had seen in the last six months. A massive buffet of gourmet looking treats was spread out before us on a long table illuminated by candles. Already many of the other guests and the Hamletville townspeople were munching on hors d'oeuvres. We had been called to the massive ballroom of the hotel. It was beautiful. The carpet had a brocade design with dark blue and gold flowers. The recessed ceiling was painted with celestial images. The wallpaper was deep blue and had spiraling silver stars inlaid. The massive chandeliers overhead twinkled beautifully. The room was arranged comfortably with small groupings of chairs and tables; they all faced a row of seats at the front.

Jamie looked hungrily at the food, but I held him back.

"Why?" he whispered.

"Did you have Mrs. May for 12th grade English?" I asked him.

He looked confused. "Yes."

"Did she make you read *The Odyssey*?"

"I think so."

"There is the story, right, where Odysseus and his men are shipwrecked on the island with the Lotus Eaters."

"Ah, yeah, I remember now. They eat lotus flowers all day long and forget home. They feel pleasure but forget everything else."

"You got it," I replied.

"But what are we going to do, fish?"

"I brought MRE's."

Jamie cringed.

"Sorry."

"The undead I can handle, but I am not sure I can take another MRE."

I smiled, taking glasses of wine for him and myself from a serving tray. "Try to look happy," I replied, "but don't drink."

"This is getting worse by the second," Jamie grumbled.

After we'd been there for just a short while, a strikingly beautiful blonde woman in an all-black jumper rang a small bell. "Everyone, please take a seat," she called sweetly, her crystalline eyes shining in the glimmering lamplight. I noticed, just for a second, a familiar lilt in her voice.

Jamie and I sat. Pastor Frank, Jeff, Summer, and Ethel sat nearest us. I noticed Frenchie was not there, and I worried. I hoped she'd played it safe and just put the girls to bed. I was surprised, however, by the number of people who were there. There were at least 75 people in the room. In that moment it seemed to me there were three groups of people there: humans, the unusual looking hotel staff, and those we suspected were vampires. I eyed the hotel staff closely. Their skin was rosy and full, but there was a strange aura about them. They seemed more beautiful, more luminescent than the rest of us, like they all had just had a great massage and facial. They intermixed freely with the vampires, not seeming the slightest bit nervous.

A few moments later, a strikingly beautiful woman in a silver sequin gown entered the room. She had waist length black hair which curled over her shoulders and down her back. Her face, though perhaps a bit past its prime, was amazingly beautiful. She had twinkling blue eyes.

She moved slowly through the crowd, her entourage circling her. Clearly, she was in charge. She smiled sweetly, welcoming the other Hamletville residents who rose when she drew near. I could tell the entire room was captivated by the woman. I didn't blame them; she was beautiful.

When she came near, I heard the accent in her voice as well. It was Slavic, perhaps Ukrainian or Belarusian. The lilt was like the same Russian accent I'd grown up with.

"Ah, here we have more newcomers. Welcome," she said as she greeted us.

"Now that's what I'm talking about," Jeff whispered as Pastor Frank introduced himself.

I noticed that the pastor had extended his hand to the woman, but she had not taken it. Instead, she simply nodded.

Ethel, Summer, and then Jeff rose to introduce themselves. I could feel the eyes of the people of Hamletville on me. They knew my concerns, and they wondered about my next move.

"Ahh, look at this," she said when she approached me. She looked me over.

Jamie and I had risen to meet her.

"It must have been so hard for you out there, eh? So many weapons."

I had gone to the party fully equipped. The guns had become so familiar a part of my wardrobe I had not thought to exclude them—especially in light of the fact that I expected, well, anything at any moment.

"What is your name?" she asked me.

"Layla," I replied.

She turned then and looked at Finn. They exchanged a glance. Again, I heard a sort of strange murmuring in my head just as I had the night Finn and Corbin had arrived in Hamletville.

"Layla," she said, considering, "Layla what?"

Lie, my instincts screamed. Lie.

"Layla Campbell."

I saw Jamie tense a little and prayed Jeff would keep his mouth shut. No one said anything.

"Well, Layla, you are safe in my house. Leave your guns in your room. I don't like them. There is nothing to fear in this place. I'll not see those guns again," she said. Then she spotted the shashka. "Now, I have not seen one of those for many years. This is yours?"

"Yeah, I found it in an antique store. I think it's a katana," I replied.

I could feel Jamie's eyes on me.

My hostess gave me a smug look. "That is called shashka," she said then turned her attention to Jamie. "And this must be your lover."

"I'm Jamie," he told her.

"Ah, James," she said and looked him over. "Handsome," she added.

She nodded to us then headed to the chairs set out in the front of the room. She took the tall, ornately designed seat at the center.

"Welcome, all of you, to the HarpWind. I am called Rumor. This is my hotel. It is my wish that you have all been brought here. We continue, every day, to seek for more survivors of this terrible disease that has killed so many. But here we are safe. We shall build a new future here. Everyone, please welcome the newcomers from—where was it," she asked, turning to Finn.

He whispered in her ear.

"Ah, yes, from Hamletville. So many survived there; they must be extraordinary people. We welcome them and shall make them part of our family. Tonight, I want you to eat your fill and feel relief. You are safe now. You are home," she said.

The crowd broke out into polite applause.

With that, someone started playing a cheerful tune on the grand piano.

"When did we get married?" Jamie whispered in my ear.

"You don't remember?" I teased.

"Well, I think I would remember my wedding night at least," he said and gave my knee a squeeze. "A katana. Seriously?"

"I liked *Kill Bill*, didn't you?"

Jamie laughed.

The crowd seemed to be enjoying themselves. Everyone was eating and drinking. Most of the Hamletville citizens looked relaxed, yet I noted some eyes were carefully taking in the scene. Buddie leaned against the bar watching every move our hosts made. I noticed that he had not eaten or drunk either. Will had come to sit near Ethel and Summer, and something in his posture seemed protective. Kiki's dark eyes roved the room suspiciously. On the other hand, Jeff had approached Matilda. He was already half drunk. He was trying to offer her a drink; he had a glass of some honey colored liquor in his hand he tried to press at her. She looked at him like she was starting at roadkill.

After a while, Rumor and her blonde companion rose and crossed the room. They were chatting in a Slavic language when they passed us. I heard Rumor call the girl Katya.

"Have you taken out the garbage?" Rumor asked.

"No, not yet. There was only one load, but Madala was there all night," Katya, the blonde woman, replied in the same language.

"Ahh, well, I shall see to it myself and decide. But get rid of the cloth," Rumor ordered.

Nodding affirmatively, the girl followed behind. "And the bogatyrka?" Katya asked with a laugh as she shot a glance back at me.

I pretended not to see.

Rumor joined her laughter. They turned then and exited the room.

I did not hear her answer.

"What is it?" Jamie whispered.

I shook my head, uncertain.

"Were they speaking Russian?" he asked.

"Some Slavic language," I replied.

"That's why you lied. What were they talking about? She looked at you and said something, bogat--?"

"She said, 'bogatyrka.' It's a very old term for a kind of female warrior."

"Layla Campbell, the bogatyrka," Jamie whispered.

I smiled wryly and wondered what Rumor had answered. I noticed then that Jamie looked pensive.

"What is it?" I asked.

"Ian."

I nodded. "Let's make one round then go."

As we circled the room, we found almost everyone talking about one thing: Rumor. Her beauty was remarkable and everyone seemed enchanted. Jamie was checking in with Mrs. Finch and Fred. I approached Buddie who was still propped against the bar.

I stood beside him. His drink was still untouched.

"Not drinking?"

Buddie inhaled deeply then turned and looked at me. "I brought my bow. I also brought several handguns and as much ammo as I could fit into a gym bag."

I raised an eyebrow at him.

Buddie nodded his chin toward the far side of the room where the piano sat.

I scanned the room. Jeff was still working on Matilda. Ambrosio had joined them. After exchanging a few words, Ambrosio and Matilda walked away from Jeff who now looked angry. Jeff tossed back his drink and sauntered over to the piano player. The piano was perched in the corner of the room near the wall. When he neared the wall, I noticed Jeff's reflection; the wall on the far end of the room was mirrored. I could also see mine and Buddie's reflections at a distance. As well, I spotted Jamie and the others. Then I saw it. Matilda and Ambrosio were crossing the room toward the door. When I looked at the mirror, however, I saw only shadows reflected there—dark, wispy shapes. I had seen those shadows before.

I looked back at Buddie.

"Now we wait," he said.

I nodded. "Now we wait."

Jamie led me down a twisting hallway of narrow corridors until we reached room 195. To our surprise, Rumor, Katya, and an unknown man were leaning over Ian. They all turned when we entered.

"Ah, here is Ms. Katana," Rumor said with a condescending smile.

The man leaning over Ian stood up. He turned and looked piercingly at us. His pale blue eyes were bulging behind thick glasses; a stethoscope hung from his neck. The three of them looked at us inquisitively.

"He's my brother," Jamie explained, motioning to Ian.

At the sound of Jamie's voice, Ian woke. "Jamie?" he called.

Jamie passed the others and took Ian's hand. Rumor sat down on the bed beside Ian. So close to her, I could smell Rumor's heavy perfume. She smelled as nice as she looked.

"How are you feeling?" Jamie asked.

Ian looked confused. "Where is Dr. Madala?"

"It's very late, Ian. He's gone to bed. I'm Dr. Rostov," the man answered.

Ian looked at Katya and then at Rumor. I could see his eyes widen as he took her in.

"These are our hosts," I explained to Ian. I was leaning against the doorframe.

"Layla? Are you there?"

"Yes, I'm here."

"You are Ian, eh?" Rumor said, taking his hand. "Oh, so strong," she added, stroking his hand. "What is the matter here?" Rumor asked Dr. Rostov.

"Cancer," he replied.

Rumor then caught sight of Ian's tattoo. "This is very unique. What does it mean?" she asked.

Ian looked toward me.

I looked at the ground, tapping the toe of my boot on the floor.

"Ian?" Rumor asked again.

He pulled his hand out from under his blanket and traced the lines of the tattoo for her. "This symbol represents a wolf," he said, tracing the shape near his shoulder. "And this shape is a doe," he then explained, tracing the shape on the lower part of the upper arm. "You see, they are entwined together. And this," he said, motioning toward the middle, "is a symbol for eternity."

"Very romantic," Rumor said thoughtfully, "the wolf and the doe."

Jamie looked at me. I could not meet his gaze.

"You will feel better soon," she told Ian then rose.

I stepped aside, clearing the door for her. She paused as she exited.

"Sergi, how does it look?" she asked the doctor in dialect. Her eyes were on Ian.

"Bad," he replied in the same.

"Fix it. I want this one," she said again in dialect.

"Da," he replied, nodding affirmatively.

She turned and looked at me. Her eyes held mine. She smiled softly, one corner of her mouth pulling into a sardonic little grin, then walked away, Katya following her. Her perfume hung in the air long after she had gone.

216

CHAPTER 26

ON THE WAY BACK TO our room, we stopped to check in on Frenchie.

"You were right, Layla," she whispered once we were inside.

"What happened?" I scanned the room. The girls were lying in bed, but they were not yet sleeping. They looked exhausted and scared.

She shook her head. "Nothing, but every eye here is on my children. There are no other kids here. We've made a terrible mistake. We need to go back."

"Something tells me they won't be inclined to allow that," Jamie told her.

Frenchie looked horrified.

I hugged her tightly then sat down on the bed beside the little girls. "Not sleeping?" I asked, tucking them in.

They shook their heads.

"Tell us a story, Layla," Kira said.

"Layla is busy, honey," Frenchie said.

"It's okay," I said, "I know a good story. It is a very old story. My grandmother used to tell it to me.

Far, far away there is a city named Kiev. Long ago, a Prince named Vladimir ruled there. The Prince put a man named Stvar in jail. Stvar often made bad decisions and talked too much. Finally his mouth got him in trouble.

When Stvar's wife, a bogatyrka named Vasilisa Nikulichna, heard the news, she knew she had to save the one she loved. She dressed like a man and put on all of her weapons. Once she got to court, she told Prince Vladimir she was a foreign prince and asked for the hand of his daughter.

Vladimir, not realizing Vasilisa was a woman, designed a number of tests to win his daughter's hand. He asked Vasilisa to best his warriors in strength. She fought hand-to-hand against the soldiers, defeating them in turn. He tested her precision. She shot her small bow longer and farther than the others. Everything was going along with Vasilisa's plan.

The Prince's daughter, however, suspected Vasilisa was a woman. She asked her father to invite Vasilisa to steam in the bathhouse. Vasilisa, however, had wit. She rushed inside the bathhouse, wet her head, and finished the bath before the Prince arrived so he never saw her body.

Thereafter, the Prince agreed to give his daughter in marriage. At the wedding, Vasilisa asked the Prince for a harp player, but the only harp player he had was Stvar. The Prince released Stvar from prison and brought him to the wedding. Once Vasilisa's husband was free, she revealed her true identity. Ashamed, the Prince let the couple go."

By the time I finished the tale, the girls had gone to sleep. I scanned the room for the mini-fridge. I rose from the side of the bed. As quietly as possible, not wanting to wake the girls, I raided the fridge.

"That stuff is long dead," Frenchie whispered as I dug around inside.

I found what I was searching for: salt. There was a small travel shaker hidden on the door. I popped it open and dumped a line of salt in front of the door leading to the hallway. Frenchie's room also had a sliding glass door that led to a balcony. I poured salt all along the entrance.

"Salt?" Jamie asked.

"Grandma Petrovich always said it keeps evil spirits away, that they can't pass salt. We can at least try," I replied.

"Thank you, Layla," Frenchie said. "I don't know what we'd do without you."

"Get some sleep. I'll be back in the morning," I told her. Then, almost as an after-thought, I pulled a vial of holy water from my vest. "Here," I said, handing it to her. "Just keep this on you. It's holy water."

"Holy water?"

I nodded.

Frenchie looked at me in amazement. "What have we done?"

I hugged her again and then Jamie and I headed to our room.

Back in the honeymoon suite, I blocked the door then sat on the side of the bed and unholstered my weapons. I pulled off my boots and clothes, leaving on a t-shirt and panties, and slid under the covers. I was exhausted.

Jamie slid into the bed beside me, and I curled up into his arms. He lay there for a long time stroking my arms, but I could tell he was preoccupied.

"What is it?" I asked.

He stroked my upper arm where I had been tattooed. The tattoo of the shashka was intermixed with other symbols, including a wolf and a doe.

"Ian never told us what the tattoo meant. I didn't know it was so personal to the two of you," he whispered.

220

"Jamie—"

"I feel like I have stolen my brother's life from him just as he is dying," Jamie said, despair filling his voice.

I rolled over and looked at him. How handsome but pained he looked. "I love my shashka ink, but otherwise the tattoos are just romantic nonsense. I want you to remember something. Ian abandoned me. Ian chose another life over a life with me. I moved on. I can't help Ian never did. He clung to the past. In the end, it was his doing that the dream ended. It was his choice. I'm not the same girl he loved."

"No," he said, stroking my hair, "you're better than that girl, Ms. Katana."

I laughed wryly. "I almost thought she was going to call me apocalypse girl."

Jamie smiled but then turned serious. "What did she say to that doctor? You understood her?"

I nodded. "She told him to fix Ian."

"That's a good thing, right?"

"I'm not sure. She said, 'I want this one.' That doesn't sound like a good thing."

"Was there something else?"

"Maybe. I don't know. In the ballroom she said something. I'm not sure what I heard."

"So far all we know for sure is she hates your guns but likes Ian," Jamie said.

"They don't cast a reflection. Buddie noticed it in the ballroom. They have no reflection—there is only a shadow," I replied.

Jamie wrapped his arms around me. "Even if they are not what they seem that doesn't necessarily mean they want to do us harm."

"When did a vampire ever want to help a human?"

"In *Twilight*."

In spite of myself, I laughed. "Yeah, well, we'll see."

CHAPTER 27

TO SAY IT HAD BEEN a long day would be an understatement. Jamie fell asleep right away, but I could not rest. I gazed down on Jamie. He was beautiful. My eyes roved over every inch and curve of his body. Desire swelled in me. I also realized how little he resembled Ian in either personality or looks. Jamie's sweetness lived on the surface. Ian's sweet side was buried deep under layers of darker elements I used to find so dangerously attractive.

As the night wore on, I lay staring at the ceiling. Heavy spring rain had begun to fall. It pounded against the windows. I felt like we were sleeping in a bear's cave. I was just waiting for the bear to wake up. The moon had traveled most of the night's sky when I started to hear strange noises coming from the floor above ours. I could hear heavy footsteps, thudding sounds, and a sound like windows opening and closing.

I rose quietly so not to wake Jamie. Snubbing the candle, I looked out the window. I saw someone walking on the roof of the porch that ran along the front of the hotel. It was a man; his movements and appearance told me it was one of them. He seemed to be looking at the upper floors. Then, crouching low at first, he jumped. He landed on one of the third floor balconies.

My heart stopped. I unbolted the window and looked out. The rain came splashing in. Apparently he heard the noise. Catching sight of me, he smiled as he leapt from one balcony to another, peeking in the windows. I knew at once who he was looking for.

"Dammit," I whispered.

I cast one look back at Jamie and was about to go back in to grab my gear when someone grabbed me by the arm and pulled me out the window. It happened so fast that I did not have a chance to call out. I landed hard on the balcony outside the room a floor below mine. Intense pain shot across my back, but every instinct inside me told me to get up.

I rose to my feet to find myself standing face to face with one of them. It was a woman; I had seen her earlier in Rumor's entourage. She was undoubtedly beautiful with long hair and large eyes. She was drenched with rain water. She grinned then lunged. She was incredibly fast. I ducked and she missed. She swung at me again; I blocked. We exchanged blows, me ducking and weaving. For a flicker of a moment I was thankful my co-worker Josephine had asked me to take jujitsu classes with her. My opponent, however, was much better at unarmed combat. With a strong side kick, she knocked me off balance. I fell backward over the balcony railing and onto the porch roof. Pain shot from one side of my head to the other. I looked up to see the man peering into what I guessed was Frenchie's room. Terror gripped my heart.

I had no time to react; she was on me again. I was still barefoot and the roof was rough under my feet. She swung again; I blocked and struck her with a hard upper-cut. She fell backward across the roof and then rolled to the ground below. With a jump, I followed her, my bare feet landing in the soft grass, mud oozing up between my toes.

Lightning shot across the sky, and a moment later there was a loud clap of thunder. Buried in the thunder-clap was the strange cat-like howl of the man who tried to creep into Frenchie's room. He had jumped backward, away from the door and onto the balcony railing, and was cradling his hand. It looked like it was smoking. With a yelp, he bounded across the balconies and disappeared back into the night.

The woman had stopped to watch the scene, a confused and worried look on her face. I took that split second to look around. In the manicured flowerbed in front of the hotel I spotted a poured concrete garden gnome. I grabbed the smiling little creature, turned, and with a heave, smashed it on the woman's head.

Clutching her head, she fell to the ground with a screech. I pounced on top of her. The massive cut I had leveled across her head and face had slowly begun to heal. I had her pinned, but she was getting better by the second. She grinned at me, her sharp teeth showing. I heaved the lawn ornament once more; then, I felt it. There was a surge of strange energy in the air then she simply poofed, transforming into a shadow. Where she had been lying beneath me there was now a black, ethereal form, a shadow. It slipped easily out of my grasp and with a twirl, it vanished into the night.

Tossing the gnome, I picked myself up and ran. I vaulted the porch railing and hit the main hotel doors. They were locked. As I yanked at the door handles, I noticed someone was inside. It was Finn. He looked up at me and smiled and waved. I turned and ran toward the door at the end of the building near the infirmary. To my luck, it was open.

I dashed down the hallway. I paused for just a moment at Ian's room. He slept soundly; no one was in sight. I ran then to the main foyer, soaking wet and still in my underwear, and up the grand stairway. Finn was no longer in the lobby.

I went at once to Frenchie's door and knocked. "Frenchie!"

"Layla?" Frenchie said sleepily as she opened the door. Once she saw my appearance, however, she was alert.

"Someone tried your window," I said and rushed across the room to check the door. It was open just an inch or two. The thunder outside boomed. When he'd pried the door open, he must have passed the line in the salt, burning his hand. I pulled the door closed and locked it.

"Who? Layla, you're soaking. And half-naked," Frenchie said.

"One of them."

Frenchie took my hand. "You're bleeding," she whispered, blotting blood off my forehead. "I'll go get Jamie."

"No."

"I'll be fast. Stay with the girls," she said then left.

A few moments after she had gone there was a soft knock on the door.

Thinking it was Frenchie and Jamie, I opened the door without hesitation. Corbin was standing on the other side.

He smiled when he saw me. I saw him take in the room; the girl's sleeping in the bed, the salt in front of the door, my half-naked self, and the nasty wound on my forehead.

"Ouch," he said, looking at the cut. "Looks like it hurts. I understand there was some commotion? May I be of assistance?" he asked.

I laughed. "Seriously? Tell your boss we want to go home. I don't want trouble. If she agrees, we'll leave peacefully."

Corbin smiled at me. His teeth were small and pointed. "You are home," he said.

"Just deliver my message like the flunky you are."

A dark shadow crossed his face, and he took a step closer toward me.

I stepped back into the room: "uh, uh, uh," I said, shaking my finger and casting a glance toward the salt.

Corbin glared at me, his face a thundercloud. He cast a glance toward the sliding glass door behind me. The first hint of morning light had appeared on the horizon.

At that same moment, Jamie and Frenchie turned the corner. Jamie had his gun drawn. He raised it at Corbin as he walked down the hall toward us.

Corbin took a long, hard look at Jamie then stalked down the hallway in the other direction.

Jamie grabbed me as he rushed into the room. "I woke up and you were gone; all your stuff was there and the window was open. Oh my god, Layla.

I thought the worst," he said, crushing me to him. "You're soaked and freezing," he added.

Frenchie crossed the room to check on the girls. They were still sleeping. She pushed the curtain aside and looked outside. "It's almost sunup," she observed.

"What happened?" Jamie whispered. He looked at the wound on my forehead. "You need stitches."

I looked back at Frenchie and the girls.

"We're okay. Go get some rest," she said.

"No, we should stay with you," I replied.

"Layla, you're hurt. Take care of yourself and then come back," Frenchie said. "In one piece."

Jamie left one of his guns with Frenchie, and we headed back to our room. The soft rays of the sun peeked over the horizon. When we got back, I sat down on the side of the bed. Jamie brought me a towel to dry my hair and found me a HarpWind Grand Hotel plush robe. The word *Bride* was embroidered on the lapel.

"This may hurt a little," he said, washing the wound with an alcohol swab.

He was right; it stung. But my whole body was already aching so it hardly mattered. More than that, I was rattled. I didn't want to be afraid, but I was. More than that, however, I was angry.

Jamie threaded a needle and, as carefully as possible, made the stitches. "You'll have a small scar. Now, tell me what happened."

I relayed the events of the night to him as he worked. I stared at his face; his eyes were glued on my forehead and the work at hand but he was listening intently. His forehead was furrowed. When he was done stitching, he cleaned the wound and dressed it with light gauze.

He looked at me, shaking his head in disbelief. "They were trying to kill you."

"I'm all right, but what do they want with Kira and Susan? Why are they so interested in those girls?"

Jamie shook his head. "I don't know. It's my fault you're here. If you had stayed back--"

"The undead might have eaten me alive, and no one would have known."

"Or you might be safe, curled up on your couch in the cabin, reading a good book."

"Queen of Hamletville, the sole survivor in a wasteland. Doesn't sound like much fun."

"Was getting tossed out of a fourth floor window fun?"

I frowned.

"Get some rest. You can't go around fighting the undead, vampires, and communing with earth spirits on no sleep. I'll keep watch," Jamie said.

"The girls . . ."

"I'll take care of it. You're not alone in this, Layla. Just rest."

I climbed into the bed. Jamie pulled the covers up and soon, despite my firm assertion I would not sleep, I was lost in dreams.

CHAPTER 28

I WOKE AROUND NOON THE next day with a blaring headache, reeling from a strange dream. In the dream I saw a mix of odd images that disturbed me. Ian was there foremost and with him were people with human bodies who had tails and heads like animals. They were all drinking cocktails. We were in a small, strange room piled high with heaps of garbage. The place smelled putrid. On some of the piles were corpses. To my shock, I turned to find Ian making love to one of the corpses. Its mouth, wide open, expelled flies each time he thrust into it. Standing beside him, a female creature with a face something like a fox or coyote laughed and stroked her own genitals as she watched. I woke feeling sick to my stomach, my head pounding.

"Here," Jamie said, handing me an aspirin and bottled water.

I looked at the pill. "Guess I better savor it. What are we going to do when pain killers run out?"

Jamie shook his head. "You're something special. I can't believe you're cracking jokes. Anyway, Buddie was by early this morning. I had him check in on Frenchie. I told him what happened last night."

"You're probably anxious to check on Ian. Let me get dressed," I said and tried to stand. The room spun wildly. I sat back down.

"When did you last eat something?"

I shrugged and sat back down. My head was killing me.

Jamie returned with a chocolate bar. "Enjoy. It's my last one," he said.

"Boy, it must be love . . . the last chocolate bar," I said then broke off a piece, handing it to him.

He smiled at me.

"I guess I should enjoy it. Between the undead trying to eat me alive and these people trying to kill me in the middle of the night, I probably don't have many meals left."

"Don't say that! Anyway, Buddie stayed for a bit this morning before he went down to keep watch on Frenchie so I could check on Ian. Ian actually looks really good. They've got an IV pumping hooked up and have started him on medications. He was looking a lot better. He was grumpy, but he seemed like he felt better."

"I hope you didn't tell him . . ."

Jamie shook his head. "No, he has other things to focus on."

I rubbed my eyes. My head still ached. And I was confused. Why were they curing Ian but trying to kill me? "We need to check on everyone, make sure everyone else is all right."

"You're in no shape to do anything. Besides, just look out the window. Half the people in the hotel are outside playing croquet."

"What?"

Jamie pulled back the curtain. I looked out at the lawn. Below I caught sight of happy people cheering as they putt croquet balls across the green. I watched Ethel cheer as her ball passed through the wicket.

"We need proof. We need to prove to them you're right. Once they believe, we'll find a way home," Jamie said.

"There is no home anymore," I said and the moment I said it, I knew it was true. Rumor would never let us leave and even if we did escape, Hamletville was the first place they would come looking. Where would we go now? Where could we hide?

Jamie reflected on my words. I could see the reality sink in with him as well. "We're out of the garden. Now we're like everyone else, looking for somewhere to be safe."

Just then, there was a knock on the door. Jamie rose to answer it. I could hear Buddie and someone else on the other side of the door. I pulled my robe on. Jamie let Buddie and Kiki in.

"How are you feeling?" Buddie asked me.

I smiled at Buddie. Like my grandma, he'd always been somewhat of a recluse, keeping to himself at his cabin by the lake. During hunting season, however, you would see a lot of him. Buddie was always the first man out of the woods, a bear or deer in tow. He would smile abashedly for his picture in the local paper. People used to talk about him, how he would take trips abroad or out west for big game hunting. Despite his efforts to avoid it, he was a good source of gossip. He would also stop by the library pretty often; I remembered him from my days hiding with Mrs. Winchester. He was quite young then. Mrs. Winchester once told him that she thought he'd read more books than anyone in town. I remembered being impressed. "Like someone kicked my ass, but otherwise fine," I replied, then smiled at Kiki.

"I left Tom with Frenchie. I told Kiki and Tom about what happened last night."

I imagined the look on Tom's face. He'd been so sure we were going somewhere safe. I could not imagine what he might be thinking now.

"Kiki noticed something I thought we should check out," Buddie added.

"I was out this morning with the others when I noticed a short-wave radio antenna on the roof of the hotel. It got me wondering who I heard when I made the transmission this winter," Kiki said. "There is something off about these people. I noticed it last night. You're right, Layla, they aren't—well, I don't know what they are. Anyway, after what Buddie told us this morning, it just made my skin turn all goose-bumps. If I can find the radio room, I might be able to see if it was them on the radio. Maybe that's how they really found us."

I nodded. "I'll get dressed."

Despite the fact my head was still aching, I stepped into the massive garden-style bathroom to pull on my clothes. Kiki and Buddie waited as I strapped on my weapons. I slid the shashka into the scabbard and attached it across my back.

"If she sees that--" Jamie said.

"She can pry it from my cold dead hands," I replied.

Buddie chuckled.

"Don't tempt her," Jamie said.

We went outside. Kiki showed us the shortwave antenna. Trying to look as inconspicuous as possible, we rounded the building looking for the antenna wire. A few seemingly normal people noticed us but didn't take an interest.

Kiki's sharp eyes scanned the building. "There," she said, motioning to the wire.

The antenna line ran across the roof and was anchored to the side of the building. It ran down the side of the HarpWind to a window on the second floor.

I grinned at the others. "Shall we?"

We entered the hotel through the maintenance entrance on the first floor and followed the stairwell to the second floor. None of us were roomed on the second floor, and no one had yet been there.

Kiki reached to push the door open, but I held back her hand.

My blood rushed to my hands, and they began to feel tingly. "Something is off here," I said. "Go careful."

Jamie pulled his gun and pushed open the heavy metal door. It opened with a click.

We entered the hallway to find it empty. It was decorated with yellow brocade wallpaper and a matching floral designed rug. A side table stood at the end of the hall. On top of it was an ornate vase with a wilted flow

We walked quietly down the hallway, listening for any sound. No one seemed to be moving.

"Do you think they sleep here?" Jamie whispered to me.

I shook my head. "Too much light," I replied. "We never see them in the daylight. Seems they avoid the sun." Large windows had flooded the hall with light on either end. We came to a cross in the hallway.

"Kiki and I can go right, you guys take the left," I said.

They nodded and we split up. Kiki and I walked carefully down the hall. We passed the laundry facilities and maid's closets. We then came to a number of administrative offices. I heard voices.

Kiki and I stopped. An office door near the end of the hall was opened. People were inside talking. Their voices were heated.

"Fine. I'll gas it up, but tell her we are low on fuel," a man said.

Pulling Kiki, we dodged into a side laundry room. We ducked low behind a heap of unwashed sheets. From the smell of the room, they had been sitting there a long time.

I saw a man storm down the hallway.

We heard someone move in the room next to us. "Have it ready by nightfall. She wants them out and back as soon as possible," the woman called behind him.

"Yeah, yeah," the man replied.

The woman had come to stand in the hallway. I could see her from my hiding place behind the laundry. She was one of those unusual people I'd seen last night. Everything about her smacked of vampire, except she seemed fully alive: rosy cheeked, beautiful, glowing. And she also seemed in the know about Rumor's plans. I wondered then what kind of unholy alliance these otherwise seemingly human people had entered into with the vampires.

Just then the radio attached to her hip blared with a loud static sound. "Office," someone called.

"Now what," she grumbled. "Go ahead."

"There are two guys creeping around on the second floor. Go chase them out, please."

"I'm on it," she replied, and with a huff, headed down the hallway where Jamie and Buddie had gone.

I slid out. When the woman turned the corner, I motioned to Kiki.

She followed behind me. We went into the office. In a room behind the main desk we saw another, smaller room. The door was just slightly ajar.

"There," Kiki whispered.

We quickly entered the small radio room. I closed the door behind us. The roof-top antenna was strung in through a window. I stood in front a mass of equipment I did not recognize.

Kiki, however, sat down and right away slid on the headphones and began adjusting dials.

"You said you did a project in school?" I whispered. Her deft hands told me that she knew more than just one project.

"I'm studying engineering at the university," she whispered. "Well, I was."

As Kiki turned the dials, I saw her listening intently. I noticed then there was a large map of the Great Lakes region taped to the wall. The map was dotted with small pins. Hamletville was marked with a red pin.

Papers were strewn across a desk. I leafed through them.

"I got something. I'm not sure what it is," she said, listening.

I leaned in and listened with her. "That's German. They are broadcasting contamination reports in German cities. You can get Germany on this radio?"

"Short-wave can pick up for thousands of miles. We didn't pick up much, but I wasn't sure if that was because our radio was so poor or if there was nothing to pick up."

She began moving dials again. I picked up a paper. On it had been written the words Barcelona Lighthouse and numbers relating to bands and kila- and mega-hurtz. I handed it to Kiki.

She adjusted several dials and then listened. After a moment, she pressed up the volume.

"Barcelona . . . Spain?" I asked.

She shook her head. "No," she said and then listened, "they are saying Barcelona Lighthouse in Westfield, New York. They are on Lake Erie," she replied, listening. "They have a looping distress call running."

I heard the static of a walkie-talkie again.

"Yeah, I'll get it. It's just over in New York. I forget the name." The woman was returning.

Kiki pulled off the headphones. I dropped the paper and pushed open the window. "Jump," I told Kiki. Following behind her, I bounced out of the window. For the second time, I landed on the roof of the porch. I did not like that this was becoming a trend. Motioning to Kiki, we ran down the porch roof against the side of the building. I waited breathlessly for the woman to shout but heard nothing. When we were a good distance from the window, I motioned to Kiki. We went to the side of the porch and carefully climbed down a flower lattice. We dropped onto the porch, surprising two older women who had been sitting there half-sleeping.

"Nice day today," I said, and grabbing Kiki's hand, we ran down the porch toward the front of the hotel.

"Oh my god, it's like they are rounding people up," Kiki said.

"Not anymore. What do we need to do to take that radio out?"

"We can pull down the antenna—that will hurt them. If I can get back into that room, I can kill the radio for good."

"That's what we need to do then," I replied. "I guess we'll need a distraction."

"Set something on fire. That always works in the movies," Kiki replied.

Kiki and I reached the front of the hotel. We scanned for Jamie and Buddie and for the right diversion.

"There," Kiki said.

I followed her gaze. There was a small building sitting near the end of the hotel.

"Looks like a lawn shed or something," Kiki added.

"Perfect, gasoline to keep it interesting and located in exactly the opposite direction of the antenna. You're good," I told Kiki.

She laughed. "Well, we Hamletville girls are hardy stock."

A moment later Ethel and Summer came up on the porch, croquet wickets in hand. They were both smiling. I wished then that our escape to the HarpWind had been just that, an escape. How different things would be now.

"Layla, honey, that lady told you to leave off your guns," Ethel said.

"I was going hunting," I replied.

"Okay, honey, just be careful," she said, patting my arm as she passed by.

"You be careful," I told her. "Both of you," I added, giving Summer a knowing glance.

She nodded and followed her mother inside.

Moments later Jamie and Buddie joined us.

"We got shooed off," Jamie said. "Had to play dumb."

"We know. We heard," I replied, and then Kiki and I told what we had discovered. We decided then to head back to Jamie and my room to hatch out a plan somewhere less public. After some discussion, we decided we needed help. That is where Will and Dusty came in. After briefing them on the full story, and watching their jaws drop, we convinced them to help. An hour later, we were ready. It was already getting late so we knew we had to hurry.

"All I get to do is yell 'fire?' That's no fun," Will said. "Let me blow something up."

"Maybe next time," I replied with a laugh.

We kept it light, but all of us knew that if anyone was caught, there would be hell to pay.

Though Dusty still seemed unclear as to why we were destroying property, he agreed to come along to cover Buddie. His eyes were wide as he'd listened to Jamie tell how they'd tried to take me out and kidnap the girls, but I could see he still was not sure what to think. I didn't blame him.

Jamie headed out to set the shed on fire while Dusty and Buddie, Buddie's bow in tow, headed to the side of the building closest to the antenna. Lucky for us, there was a stand of trees on the antenna end of the hotel. From there, Buddie could make a shot. He'd secured a metal line to one of his arrows and had a small winch he was going to use as a make-shift pulley to bring the antenna down.

"I only get one shot," Buddie said as he showed us his creation.

"I'm not worried. You'll be accurate," I smiled encouragingly.

Kiki and I headed to the employee stairwell again. To our luck, no one was around. We jotted down the same hallway to our hiding spot in the laundry room without detection.

Then, we waited. After a while we heard yelling. Will.

Static on the walkie blared. "Front desk, what's all that noise?" we heard a man ask.

"The god damned shed is on fire," someone replied through static.

"Fuck," I heard the man swear.

"Better get on it. She'll be up soon," a woman replied.

A moment later we saw a man storm down the hallway.

"Complication," I whispered to Kiki and motioned for her to stay hidden.

I slid out of the room and snuck a look into the office. The woman we had seen earlier was sitting there looking at some papers. Her back was toward me. There was only one option. Moving quickly, I rushed the room, grabbed the woman by the back of the head and slammed her head on the desk. Knocked unconscious, she fell to the floor.

I motioned Kiki. We ran into the radio room.

"Let me cut power," Kiki said and then, with a knife and screwdriver in hand, Kiki slid under the table. A moment later, the lights on the radio went dim. She then started pulling wires and breaking something that sounded like glass. She slid back out from under the table and looked the radio over. She grinned. "Kill the antenna," she told me.

Unsheathing the shashka, I cut the wire. Kiki then pulled a couple of small electrical components out of the radio, sticking them in her pocket, and smiled at me. "Done," she said.

"That was easy," I answered.

Just then, we heard a loud crashing sound coming from outside. There was a tug on the wire running through the window. Moments later, the wire zipped away.

"Let's go," I whispered.

We ran down the hallway toward the employee stairwell. When we opened it, however, we heard noise coming up from below. We closed the door and headed down the hall in the other direction but voices rose coming toward us.

"Try the doors," I whispered to her, but they were all locked.

At the last moment, I spotted the dumbwaiter in the wall. I grabbed Kiki. If either Kiki or I had weighed a pound more, we would not have fit into the commercial sized dumbwaiter. I pulled the door closed. At once we could feel we were dropping.

"Our weigh is pulling us down," Kiki whispered.

The dumbwaiter lowered us gently to the first floor. I pushed open the door just enough to look out. We were in the kitchen adjacent to the ballroom. A number of people, including the odd looking hotel staff, were moving around preparing dishes.

I motioned to Kiki. There was a serving cart near us.

"You get under," she whispered and then pointed to a chef's jacket lying on top of the cart. "I'll push."

Moving quickly, we slid out of the waiter. Pushing the curtains on the cart aside, I hid under the cart. Kiki ducked low, pulled the jacket on, and then stood up and began to roll the cart from the room. I heard her set dishes on top.

We were near the exit when I saw feet approach Kiki.

"Where do you think you're going?" a man asked her.

"Step off. I need to take this upstairs. Now."

"For what?"

"For what? What do you think? *She* asked it be sent up. Why don't you go ask *her*," Kiki replied in her bitchiest tone.

"Leave the cart downstairs. You can take the tray up," the main replied.

"And you can fix my broken back. I'll push it to the stairs and bring the cart back when I'm done. Now move," Kiki said and with a shove of the cart, set off out of the kitchen.

She pushed the cart down a series of winding halls and after a few moments, she stopped. She pushed the curtains aside. "Come on," she whispered.

She'd pushed the cart into a closet. She pulled off the jacket and put it and the wine decanter and glasses she'd set on top of the cart into the trash.

We then walked, as nonchalantly as possible, across the main foyer and back up to my and Jamie's room. Jamie and Will were already waiting inside. Jamie and I shared a glance, both relieved the other was safe.

"It's done," Kiki said.

Then we waited.

"Maybe I should have brought the wine," Kiki said. Moments later Buddie and Dusty arrived.

"No problems," Buddie said. "It just made a hell of a noise coming down."

"They came running, but no one spotted us," Dusty added.

"But they will suspect us—you," Buddie said to me.

"Yeah, but it was worth it. God knows how many others we just saved."

"Maybe you should have just blown up the boat," Dusty said.

"I'm not planning on swimming home," Will told him.

Jamie and I exchanged a glance but said nothing. After more than an hour passed and we heard nothing, the others went back to their rooms and Jamie and I headed downstairs to check on Ian.

It was now dark out. *They* were awake and moving around. Their piercing eyes bore into me.

"Maybe we should have stayed back," Jamie whispered.

"Doesn't matter. They'd know where to find me."

We found Ian sitting up in bed, the IV still attached to him.

"Ahh, here is the happy couple," he said when we entered, startling both of us. Ian looked much better. His skin was looking less thin, his eyes less sunk in, the dark rings around them gone. "I thought you had forgotten me," he added.

Jamie shook his head. "Never, little brother. How are you feeling?"

"They have been pumping me full of shit all day," Ian said, looking down at the IV. "I don't even know what all they got going into me, but I'm feeling good. Christ, Layla, what happened to your head? Rough sex?"

I had removed the bandage earlier, but the fresh stitches were still evident on my forehead. .

"Hey brother, no need for that kind of talk," Jamie told Ian. Jamie looked as perplexed as I felt.

"Yeah, yeah, whatever. They ever feed anyone around here?" Ian asked.

"Let me go see if I can get you something," Jamie said and then left the room.

I sat down beside Ian and reached into my vest pocket where I had hidden the last piece of the chocolate bar Jamie had given me. I handed it to him.

Ian laughed sardonically but ate all the same. "Geez, Layla, you're so generous," he said.

"You saw the doctor today?"

"Yeah, they've got me on all kinds of meds. Rostov was just here. Creepy dude."

I nodded.

"Hey Layla, when did you decide to go after Jamie? Before or after you spent all winter toying with me?"

"I never toyed with you. We are friends."

"Be my friend but fuck my brother, that's nice."

"Almost as nice as you did me, right Ian?"

Ian looked down at his hands and played with the candy wrapper. "Yeah, you're right about that," he muttered.

Jamie returned. "They are bringing you dinner, brother," he said and then spotted the chocolate wrapper. "You need anything else?" Jamie asked.

Ian looked piercingly at me. "I guess not," he said bitterly.

Jamie picked up on the tone. "We'll check back in later. Why don't you get some rest," he said. Jamie took my hand, and we made our way out of the room.

"Going back to *your* room, eh? Yeah, you two go ahead," Ian called after us then laughed harshly.

I led Jamie outside, and we sat on a bench on the porch. The moon cast white light on the dark lake waves. The air was cool but smelled clean. The sweet scent of spring flowers and new growth perfumed the air. When you weren't fighting for your life or performing demolition, the view was actually rather peaceful. Jamie was quiet. Only a few of the lanterns on the porch had been lit. In the shadow, I could see Jamie was upset.

"I'm sorry. I shouldn't have shared your gift with him," I said.

"No, no," Jamie said, picking up my hand and kissing my fingers, "bless your kind heart. It's just . . ."

"It's not him talking, you know that, it's the medications and the illness. He's not himself."

"I'm sorry he spoke to you like that."

I had to laugh. "He has spoken much worse to me, believe me."

"It's not right."

"Well, it is what it is."

We sat there for a long time, the moon climbing high in the sky. I could sense Jamie was feeling ashamed about going back to the room we shared together. I understood, so we sat and took in the moonlight even though all of my senses were on edge. The feel of danger was all around me. After a while, we decided to go look at the water. We found a quiet spot and sat watching the moonlight reflecting on the waves. A distance away from the hotel, I felt better. The view was beautiful.

Late into the night, we decided to head back. We were crossing the lawn to the hotel when we heard the yacht's horn sound. We turned to see the boat headed toward the hotel. It pulled into the pier then sounded the horn twice more. From our view we could see a flurry of activity on board.

"Did they bring more survivors after all?" Jamie asked, straining to get a look.

"I don't know, but something's up," I replied, regretting I'd left my binoculars in the room.

One of the crewmen bounced out of the boat before the plank had been lowered and ran, quickly, across the hotel lawn.

Concerned, Jamie and I headed toward the pier. They were dropping the plank for a small group of about five or six very normal but war-torn looking survivors. Behind them two men rushed the body of a female back toward the HarpWind.

Jamie and I had just reached the end of the pier as they passed us. The woman they carried was bleeding profusely from a wound on her side. From her appearance, I knew her to be a vampire. Now I was confused.

"She's not going to make it," one of the men said.

They stopped and laid the woman on the ground. Then they both just stood over her. No one did anything. The new arrivals watched in horror as the woman lay on the ground, jerking and bleeding, seemingly dying.

"Isn't someone going to do something?" one of them whispered.

"Do something," Jamie told the two men.

They looked blankly back at him.

"What happened?" I asked the survivors.

"We aren't exactly sure. We think one of our people who got sick grabbed her. We didn't see it happen," a man told me.

"Christ," Jamie swore and pulled some medical gloves from his pocket. He started pulling them on.

"She's one of them. You know that, right?" I whispered to him.

He nodded and bent down to look at the woman.

"Don't do that," one of the men said, but no one moved to stop him.

Jamie ripped the woman's shirt away to reveal a nasty wound on her side. It was clear she had been bitten. As Jamie cleaned the wound, I kneeled down beside him. The woman breathed hard, blood sputtering from her lips. Her body twisted.

Jamie took the woman's hand. He felt her wrist. "No pulse," he whispered to me, but the woman was clearly moving.

We both looked at the injury. I remembered how it looked when April turned. This was not the same thing. I didn't know what I was seeing. It was almost as if her body as trying to heal itself, and at the same time, the infection fought her. The battle seemed to have been going on for a while. Moments later, we watched as the wound finally sealed itself closed. Then, something strange happened. The woman's moon-like white skin started to regain color. Her pale skin took on a rosy, healthy glow. We watched as it spread across her stomach and up her neck to her face. Her lips turned pink, and the blush of life came to her cheeks. Her eyes closed. A

253

moment later, she opened them again. They were now hazel colored. She lifted her hand and wiped the blood away from her mouth, grimacing at the taste.

Jamie took her arm again, his fingers pressed against her wrist.

The next moment I felt a tug on the back of my pants, and then, startling all of us, heard a gunshot.

The woman jerked.

I jumped up and turned to find Rumor standing there with my gun in her hand. She was wearing a long, golden ball-gown, the trimming barely hiding her breasts. The gun in her hand made for a stark contrast.

Jamie and I looked at the injured woman; the shades of life momentarily back in her face were now frozen in the grimace of death. Rumor had shot her between the eyes.

"I guess it is a good thing you ignored me after all," she said, handing me back my gun. "You're very useful to have around. Why would I ever let you go home," she motioned to the others to take the woman away.

"Welcome, all," she said to the newcomers. "Where have you come from?"

"New York, Westfield area," a woman said.

"Go inside. You're safe here," she said and motioned the newcomers to the hotel. She then motioned for Jamie and me to follow her.

We walked behind her. A crewman walked at her side. "What happened?" she asked, switching to dialect.

"She bit into one of the infected. She didn't know. Then it attacked her," he replied in the same.

"I told you all to be careful."

"We're sorry."

"You're sorry, but I was the one who had to shoot her. Let's not be sorry next time."

"Da," he replied abashed.

"Of course, maybe there will be no more survivors now that someone has taken out the radio," she said, switching back to English. She did not look back at us, but I knew where her comment was directed.

When we got to the door, Rumor stopped. She looked at Jamie. "Thank you for trying to help my friend," she said and then went inside leaving Jamie and I to stand looking at each other not knowing what to think. I told Jamie what she had said.

"That woman had no pulse when I knelt down. She was as dead as a corpse. But after she turned, I felt her blood. She had a pulse. It was like her heart had started again."

"The blood," I said, "the undead blood revived her?"

Jamie shook his head. "I don't know, but . . ."

I looked back at the boat.

"What does it mean?" he asked.

"I don't know."

The rest of the night passed uneventfully. I don't know if Rumor decided I was too dangerous to mess with, had another plan waiting for me, was expressing true gratitude toward Jamie, or had just taken the night off, but neither I nor Frenchie were disturbed that night. I knew I should stay awake. I knew I should try to figure out what to do next, but my body could bear no more. Adrenaline can only take you so far. After all, I was human. I lay down that night in Jamie's arms and slept soundly.

CHAPTER 29

EARLY THE NEXT MORNING THERE was a sharp rap on the door. "Layla," I head Tom call. "Layla . . . Jamie," he called again, knocking hard.

I jumped out of bed and unbarred the door, flinging it open.

Tom, looking frantic, was on the other side. "You need to come quickly," he said.

Jamie was just rolling out of bed. "Is it Ian?"

Tom shook his head, and then noticing our state of undress, looked away, embarrassed. "Sorry, guys," he said, "but it's urgent."

Jamie and I slid our clothes on and grabbed our weapons. Rushing outside, the three of us crossed the nicely manicured lawns of the HarpWind Grand to the lakeside. There, the HarpWind was poised at the edge of a cliff 40 feet above the water. Several people leaned against a fence and looked below. I noticed that Dusty and Buddie were there; they both looked very upset.

As I walked toward the fence, my blood began to cool. Jamie and I looked over. There, far down on the rocks below, lay the body of Pastor Frank.

"I was out walking," Buddie said, "when I saw him there."

Just then a group of five people from the hotel ran across the lawn and joined us.

"What is it?" a woman with wild curly red hair asked. She looked over the side.

"Another accident," a bystander answered. She had been standing by Dusty and Buddie when Jamie, Tom, and I had arrived. I looked at her. She was an older woman, about seventy or so, with curly gray hair.

The red-haired woman instructed the two men with her to go down and get the body.

"I'm coming too," I said, joining them. The others from Hamletville were fast on my heels.

"Oh, it's okay, we can take care of it," she replied.

"I said I'm going. We all are," I told her sternly, and we followed the two men as they wound down a narrow flight of stairs on the cliff-side. When we got to the bottom, we jogged over to Pastor Frank's body. The cold lake waves were breaking on his feet. He lay face down.

Buddie leaned down and turned him over. His face was frozen in the grimace of death. He was pale white, his skin tinged blue around the edges.

His eyes, a sort of light golden brown color, were alarmingly wide open.

I heard Dusty inhale sharply.

Jamie leaned down and closed the Pastor's eyes. He turned and looked up at me.

"What happened?" Tom wondered aloud.

One of the two men looked back up at the others standing by the fence. "Must have slipped. Ground is still wet. If you're not careful, it's really easy to fall."

I looked at the man. Did he really think we were that stupid?

"That's why you have a fence though, isn't it?" Buddie asked, and I watched his eyes work. He was calculating: distance, trajectory, broken vegetation, injuries. When he was done, he looked at me. Buddie shook his head.

I nodded.

The two men bent to pick up Pastor Frank's body.

"Here, let us," Dusty said, grabbing the Pastor's shoulders. Jamie took his legs and Buddie, Tom, and I followed behind. The two men led us back up the stairs. At the top, Jamie and Dusty, each out of breath, lay the body down.

The red-haired woman kneeled and looked over the pastor. "I'm sorry," she told us. "There is a garden in the back of the hotel. We've been interring people there as needed."

Buddie had moved away from the group and was examining the cliff edge.

"You have that need a lot?" I asked.

She looked sharply at me. "People have come with injuries, diseases, as I am sure you can guess. You were out there. You know what it was like. Unfortunately, some guests haven't made it."

She motioned to the men to take Pastor Frank. "We'll see to him," she said.

They left then, taking the body with them.

I went to the older woman who was standing with the other bystanders. Her eyes had welled with tears. "Such bad luck," she said, setting her hand on my arm. "He was a priest, wasn't he? That is so unfortunate. We didn't have any men of the holy cloth here until he arrived."

The holy cloth. "You said, *another* accident?"

She nodded. "I was here on vacation when the outbreak began. I've seen so many newcomers found—it's wonderful—but there have been a few unfortunate accidents. It's so sad, to endure so much and then die in a fall or the like. Truly a shame. I'm sorry for your loss," she told me and patted my arm. She turned, and with a small group of others, headed back to the hotel.

I joined Tom, Jamie, and Dusty. Buddie joined us a moment later. "He definitely did not slip and fall," Buddie told us.

I gazed out at the lake. Beautiful pink and purple clouds, the last of the shimmering sunrise, were just dissipating.

"What do you mean?" Tom asked Buddie.

"I mean, however he died, it wasn't like they said it was."

They looked at me. I shook my head, not knowing what to say. I guess Rumor got her payback after all.

Jamie looked worried. "I need to check on Ian."

I nodded. "Let's make sure everyone else is accounted for," I said, pulling the list of room numbers from my pocket.

"We'll get it," Dusty said, nodding to Buddie and taking the list from my hands.

"Who is with Frenchie? Tom, can you go check on her and the girls? I want a look at Pastor Frank's body. Maybe I can figure out what really killed him," I said.

Tom nodded, and he, Buddie, and Dusty headed back to the hotel.

Jamie took me by the arm. "Wait for me."

"Ian is so vulnerable. He needs you with him," I replied. "I'll be fine. I'll come as soon as I get some answers. Besides, it's daytime," I said.

Jamie pulled me into a quick kiss, and we headed off in opposite directions. I went east, following the direction they had taken Pastor Frank.

They'd gone around the side of the hotel toward the back.

As I rounded the side of the island, I kept one watchful eye on the HarpWind and another on the nearby grounds. It was still very early, and the mist was just clearing. In some places it was still quite foggy. I'd been walking past rows of small ponds when the mist got thick. The hair on the back of my neck rose, and I felt the familiar buzz of the supernatural in the air. Carefully, I sought for the cliff-side to orient myself. As I neared it, the mist cleared. I could see very thick vegetation growing in a sloping angle toward the water, not a drop-off like the front of the hotel. And then, in the distance, for just a moment, I spotted tall trees that seemed to emerge from the lake. Then, the brush rustled.

I pulled my sword.

A moment later a red fox appeared before me. She sat and looked expectantly at me. I knew at once the creature was not what she seemed. "Go ahead. I'll follow," I told her.

She trotted into the brush. At first it looked like I would need to slash a path through the thicket, but then I noticed some very old, eroded wooden stairs embedded in the slopping earth.

Pushing the thicket aside, I followed her.

Low to the ground, the fox bolted easily through the thickets. I, on the other hand, had to push my way through. Scratched from head to toe and covered in cobwebs, I finally emerged in a swampy area. High cattails grew there. I looked back. Only the roof of the HarpWind was visible.

Sitting on a grassy tuft, the fox waited. Once I'd turned to her, she led me across the wet terrain. Moments later we emerged on the rocky shoreline. In the distance were the tall trees I had spotted. They were on a small island that was, perhaps, fifty feet from the shore of Enita Island.

The fox bounced across the rocky shoreline to an old rowboat that sat on the rocks. She crawled inside and sat on the bench.

I walked over to the boat. There were oars inside.

"Are you sure?" I asked her.

She laid down.

I pushed the boat into the water and hopped in, expecting the old thing to sink at any minute. It didn't. I pulled out the oars and rowed toward the neighboring island.

Within ten minutes, the prow of the rowboat slid onto the gravel shoreline.

The fox hopped out and waited for me.

I jumped out and dragged the boat ashore. The island was very small but was dotted with exceptionally tall pine trees. The shoreline where we had landed was pebble, slopping upward to a very high bank.

The fox turned and headed up the bank into the woodsy area. I followed. The grass at my feet mixed with rocks and pine needles. A fresh, earthy smell filled the early spring air. We walked clockwise around the island until we reached the side furthest from the hotel. There the fox turned toward the center of the island. After a few moments, we came to a clearing.

I was standing at the top of some earthen steps that loomed about eight feet above a circular pit at the island's center. The tall pine trees grew in a circle around the pit. From this vantage, I found myself looking down on a labyrinth. Stones had been set into the ground in a circular pattern that looked like a coiled snake. At the center was the head. A long, snaky tongue extended from its mouth, spiraling with increasing smaller stones. The entrance to the labyrinth was at the bottom of the stairs. There, round rocks, resembling a snake's rattle, were piled.

The fox looked back at me and headed into the labyrinth.

I took a deep breath and followed.

As I wove around the circle, I could feel the energy rising. It was that same strange feeling I'd felt before but something about it seemed more intense, wilder. A pulsing feeling of electricity made my ears ring almost painfully. The chaotic energy made my skin itch. With each step I took I felt it even more.

As I neared the center, my heart started racing. The island's tall trees loomed overhead. Moments later, I stood close to the center. I stopped before I reached the head of the snake. The fox trotted into the space in front of me and then, before my eyes, shifted into the guise of a human woman. She wore leather pants and boots and blousy cotton shirt. Her hair was dark, but the sun's ray breaking through the trees gave her hair a reddish hue. She wore a bow strapped across her chest and a dagger hung from her belt. Her face was painted on one cheek; three lines blended into a circular solar image. She stood very near the center of the spiral.

"Welcome to Ëde-ka Island," she said.

I nodded in respect.

"Ëde-ka means sun. Here," she said, motioning to the labyrinth, "you stand at the heart of the sun, at the head of the snake."

"The other island, Enita, which is the moon?"

She nodded. "The moon, the crescent. That is why the usurpers have taken the island; they are creatures of darkness. But they have bastardized that sacred lunar space," she said angrily. "Here, however, they can touch nothing. The sun is their enemy."

"They are vampires?" I said.

"That is what you call them. They are not from this land. They came from abroad and took over this holy space."

I looked back toward the HarpWind. It was a shadow in the distance.

"You must leave this place," she told me.

"They won't let us just walk off."

"No sooner than the hunter lets the rabbit off the spit. It will need to destroy them. This place, however," she said, motioning to the labyrinth, "is a doorway. We have long kept such doors secret, locked to your kind. But we are in a new world now. Destroy them, and our doors will be unlocked to you. Complete the spiral," she said, motioning to the snake's tongue, "and you will pass through the door."

"Did Peryn send you?"

She cocked her head and looked at me. "Peryn?"

"Peryn, the forest spirit. She's like you, right?"

The woman simply looked at me.

"Why are you helping us?" I asked.

"You are now on the fringe just as we are, just as those dark creatures are," she said, motioning back to the HarpWind. "But the outcome is still unclear. Your kind has finally gone entirely windigo. Yet some of you still remain. We are not sure why," she said.

"The gateway, where does it lead?" I asked.

She half-smiled then. "We shall meet again, I think," she said, then turned, morphing back into a fox. She trotted to the center of the spiral and disappeared.

The unanswered question hung in the air.

CHAPTER 30

BY THE TIME I GOT back to Enita Island it was nearly noon. I knew Jamie would be worried, but I could not let the issue of Pastor Frank's death go.

I made my way to the back of the hotel and found the small garden they were using as a cemetery. I noticed right away that no graves were marked, there were no crosses, and there were at least thirty bodies buried there.

The two men who had taken Pastor Frank's body were dropping the final shovels of dirt on a fresh grave. They looked up when I approached them.

"I want to see the Pastor's body," I told them.

One of them smiled sardonically and turned away. The other looked piercingly at me. "He is here," he said, looking down.

"You buried him already?"

The man didn't have to answer me.

I bit my tongue cutting off every sarcastic remark that wanted to leap from my mouth. The less they suspected I knew, the better. I turned and left, ignoring the low sounds of their chuckles. They would get theirs.

Back in the hotel, I wound my way through the halls toward the infirmary. I arrived at Ian's room to find him sitting up. He looked really good, very healthy. His IV stand, however, was hung with two bags: one was clear, and the other looked like blood.

"What is this?" I asked him, staring at the IVs.

"One has chemo medicine. The other is a blood transfusion. They gave me one yesterday too. They said it would help me build up my white blood cells."

My hands started tingling.

"Rumor came by to see me last night after you and Jamie left. She was really interested in you. Man, her tits are something else."

I frowned. My head was spinning.

"Oh, come on, Layla. I didn't tell her anything."

I stared at Ian. Was my mind playing tricks on me? He already looked different. "No, I'm sure you didn't, it's just--"

"I can hear my blood thundering in my veins," he interrupted. "Two days ago I felt like I was on death's doorstep. Now I just want to . . . I don't know what. My head is full of weird ideas."

I clutched the frame of the door and inhaled deeply.

"Layla?"

I looked at Ian again. His sweet blue eyes had already started to lose some of their pigment. My words were lost. I did not know what to say to him. My head spun. I rushed out of the room.

"Layla?" I heard him call.

I ran down the hallway.

"Layla!"

I ran outside and burst into a sob. After a few moments, I felt someone approach me.

"Are you all right?" the man asked. I noticed he was wearing a stethoscope.

"Are you Dr. Madala?" I asked, wiping away my tears.

He nodded.

"I'm Layla. I'm Ian's . . . sister-in-law. Can we talk?"

The doctor suddenly looked uncomfortable. He looked around. "Not here," he said and led me back inside. Just inside the door there was an office. The doctor unlocked the door, and we went in. He closed and locked the door behind him.

"You were the doctor who saw Ian the night we arrived?"

"Yes, I was."

"And what was your prognosis at the time?"

The doctor looked at me. I could tell by the expression on his face he already knew what I was getting at. "He was in the advanced stages of cancer."

"How have you been treating him?"

"Chemotherapy, mostly," he said.

"Did you put him on the blood transfusions?"

The doctor looked at his hands then back at me. "No, Dr. Rostov started that round of treatment yesterday."

"Isn't there a third doctor here? They told us there were three."

The doctor rested his hand on his forehead. "She had an accident."

"I see," I said looking closely at him. "Let's be frank."

The doctor sat back in his chair.

"Is there any hope for Ian?"

The doctor shook his head. "He'll become one of them."

"Why are you helping them?"

"I *am* curing people. I *am* helping the sick who are brought here. It's just, after they leave my hands . . . Look, either I help them or they kill me."

"How long have you been here?"

"Almost five months."

"What are they doing with these people? Eating them? Killing them?"

"Many here are pets. Rumor and the others drain them just a little, drink some of their blood, enjoy their bodies. In exchange, the pets get a little of the vampiric gift, a small dose of the blood. It gives them beauty, strength, health, longer lives. It is a deal many choose to make. Especially in these days."

"Not you?"

"Not me. I once enjoyed being human."

"And what about Ian?"

"Ian is now a pet whether he knows it or not. But I understand it is Rumor's intention to offer immortal life."

My stomach shook. "I need your help. Please, talk to my people. They need to see these creatures for what they are before it's too late. I need to get my people safe, and until they believe me, I can't do that. Please, they will believe you. Please talk to them."

"Every eye in this place is already on you. They watch your every move. I can do nothing for you without risking myself. It is a risk just talking to you."

"What if we take Ian off the blood?"

"The cancer will return and kill him."

"We saw something strange. The blood of the undead seemed to, well, it seemed to make one of Rumor's people return back to their mortal self. Maybe Ian--"

"No," Dr. Madala interrupted. "You're right. It will return him to a mortal life, but he will return fully intact and with whatever mortal ailments he once carried. The vampiric seed only provides its healing power while he carries its magic. Becoming a vampire does not, as we were lead to believe, kill you. It simply transforms you to another state of existence, something different from human."

"Just like the undead."

"Yes, just like them."

I stood. "Then there is no hope for Ian."

"I'm sorry."

I turned and walked out. Standing in the hallway, I looked toward Ian's room. I had once loved Ian with every fiber of my being. I had wanted to be his wife, to bear his children. The echo of that love had thundered loudly when I had first arrived in Hamletville almost seven months ago, but it had become clear almost immediately that it was just that—an echo. I had once loved him, but that is all. In place of that love was fondness stemming from our shared history. I'd once thought him my soul-mate, but he betrayed me. Ian didn't choose the vampire blood, but his change betrayed all of us. It was truly too late. And while it made me sad, I felt even sadder for the great loss Jamie would feel . . . Jamie, who had never betrayed anyone.

I stepped back outside and took a deep breath. Jamie needed to know. I headed toward the front of the hotel, but Will intercepted me.

"Oh my god! There you are," he said breathlessly.

"What is it?" I asked, wiping a tear from my eye.

"Kira and Susan are missing!"

My heart skipped a beat. We rushed back to Frenchie's room. When we entered, I saw Frenchie's face and eyes were red. Buddie was talking to her in a quiet tone. Jamie stood over them. Summer and Tom were sitting on the bed listening.

Everyone looked up when I entered.

Frenchie collapsed into tears. I went to her side and put my hand on her shoulder.

"She took them outside for some air. Kira dropped her bear in one of the fountains. Frenchie reached down to get it and when she got back up, the girls were gone," Jamie told me.

"I came back hoping they were here," Frenchie sobbed. "Layla, I looked everywhere." Frenchie's voice was hoarse from screaming.

"How long ago?" I asked.

"Maybe twenty minutes," she whimpered.

"Dusty went back to the fountains to check again," Buddie told me.

"Boots on the ground. In pairs. We need everyone. Now," I said.

Tom and Summer nodded and headed out of the room. I could hear them knocking on doors in the hallway followed by the sound of Hamletville voices. Soon there was a flurry of movement.

"Can you track them?" I asked Buddie.

"Let's see," he replied, and the four of us headed back to the garden where Frenchie had last seen her daughters. It was a beautiful place, full of fresh spring tulips, the air perfumed with hyacinth. The fountains shimmered in the sunlight.

Jamie and I stood aside as Frenchie talked and Buddie scanned the ground.

"Where have you been?" Jamie asked.

There was too much to tell. "Later," I whispered.

Jamie looked inquisitively at me, but just then Dusty came up to us. "No sign," he whispered.

Buddie went over the ground looking again and again. He shook his head. "I see tracks in, nothing out."

Frenchie sobbed.

I took her hand. "We'll find them."

I scanned the horizon. Two girls could not vanish into thin air. We set off in groups and began searching the island. By late afternoon, no one had seen anything. Getting together as many of the Hamletville people as we could, we regrouped in Frenchie's room. No one had seen any sign of the girls.

"Maybe we should tell the hotel staff," Ethel suggested.

"No, no way," Dusty said. "They took those girls."

Ethel looked shocked. "Are you sure?"

Everyone was looking at one another. By now they had all heard someone had tried to kill me and about Pastor Frank's accident. This, coupled with the news of Kira's and Susan's disappearance, had everyone on edge. Not only that, they also had heard reports from the other hotel guests. Others related tales of accidents and odd disappearances.

"Layla?" Tom said.

The entire room looked at me. I could tell from the pained expressions on their faces, they knew I had been right.

"We need to find Kira and Susan then we need to get out of here," I said.

Several people nodded.

"What is happening here? What are these people?" Ethel asked.

I looked at Jamie and gave him a *should we tell them* expression.

He looked as uncertain as I did. "They're vampires," he said at last.

Several people in the group looked stunned.

Jeff laughed out loud. "That is the stupidest thing I've ever heard. Vampires don't exist."

"Just like that zombie that tried to chew your foot off last week doesn't exist, right?" Kiki said stingingly.

"Have you seen Ian? He looks so much better. They *are* helping us," Mrs. Finch said.

276

I looked at Jamie. We hadn't talked yet, so I said nothing.

"Yeah, just like they helped Pastor Frank off the cliff," Buddie replied.

"Or helped Layla out the fourth floor window," Jamie added.

"Or helped us come here by tracking us on the radio," Kiki said.

Several people in the group still looked unsure.

"Look," Tom said, "you all know I wanted to come here more than anyone, but Layla was right. You can feel it, right? It's that same bad feeling you get when you walk home alone in the dark, or when you are in a room and can sense someone else is there. I used to get that feeling all the time when I fought fires, like something was squeezing my throat. Don't you all feel it too?" he asked them. "We can't see what it is, but she can," he said, looking at me. "We have to trust Layla."

"We're a few days too late," Ethel said.

"We're still alive," I replied.

"It's all there. You just have to look. They cast no shadow. They don't walk in the daylight. They don't eat food. They *look* wrong," Buddie said.

I could see by the overwhelming fear and despair on their faces, they had been convinced.

"We have to find those girls," Summer whispered.

It occurred to me that wherever they had Kira and Susan, it was some place we had not yet seen, some place where the hosts were sleeping during the day.

"We will find them, and we will get out of here. We need to keep looking, but we also need to get ready. Is the bar well stocked?" I asked, turning to Jeff.

He looked confused but nodded. "It's huge."

"We need bottles. Hard liquor. As much as you can get. Can you do that?"

He nodded.

"I'll help," Will offered.

"You all need to play it cool. Keep to yourselves. Tomorrow morning, dawn, after they go to sleep, we'll torch this place and go. We just need to make it through the night," I said.

"What if we don't find them by then?" Frenchie asked.

"We'll find them."

We made a plan to round up supplies and people. Everyone would meet at the front porch on the eastern end of the hotel at dawn. Several of us broke into groups to go looking for the girls, but it was late afternoon, and there was less than an hour of daylight left.

Jamie made me promise to check on Ian again while he and Tom went out once more to look for the girls. It was not a trip I was looking forward to making.

When I got to the infirmary, Ian was sitting on the side of his bed staring at his hands. The I.V. was gone. He had redressed in clothes I did not recognize. When he turned to look at me, I froze. His blue eyes had totally lost their pigment and had changed to an icy color. It was not just the color of his eyes that startled me but what I saw lying behind them. It was not Ian who looked out at me but his shadow aspect—his dark, angry self. I had seen glimpses of that side of him before and feared it. Once, long ago, he'd drunk too much at a party and thought I was paying too much attention to another man. On the way back to the car, he'd hit me. He was sorry later, but now he had the same look in his eyes. I knew then the transformation he had made was not just a physical one. His id had slipped its chain.

"Layla," he said, "I was just thinking about you."

"You're looking much better, Ian," I replied carefully.

He smiled at me. "It's strange, isn't it," he said then looked again at his hands, turning them over and back. "I feel perfectly fine. In fact, I feel really good. Come sit by me," he said and patted the bed beside him.

I felt my spine stiffen, but I went all the same.

He turned and looked at me, brushing the hair away from my face. "You look worried," he said.

"Kira and Susan are missing."

He frowned. "Maybe they will be at the party tonight," he said absently.

"What party?" I asked.

Ian then slid his hands up my arms. He pushed my shirt sleeve up to reveal the tattoo on my arm and shoulder. "Once upon a time, we were one," he said, looking at the tattoo. His hands tightened on my arms. "Now you're fucking my brother."

"Ian," I began, but with exceptional speed and strength, he pushed me onto the bed and laid on top of me, stuffing his hand down the front of my pants while he squeezed the tattoo on my arm. He shoved his hand hard into my panties and then into the soft folds of my flesh, pressing his fingers into my body.

"Ahh," he groaned as he thrust his fingers deeper inside me, rubbing his crotch against my body. "Come on, Layla. You're letting Jamie fuck you all night long. At least you can blow me one more time," he said as he leaned in, whispering in my ear.

With my free hand, I pulled my gun from its holster and leveled the barrel on Ian's forehead.

Startled, he opened his eyes.

I pulled the lever back. "How about I blow your brains across the ceiling?"

He leapt away from me. Seconds later he was standing in the middle of the room. I centered the gun on him.

He grunted. "Fuck you. Let Jamie have you then," he said and walked out of the room.

I rose and looked out the door. Ian had already passed the length of the hallway. The door leading outside banged closed. He was gone.

CHAPTER 31

I FOUND JAMIE ALONE IN our room. He had been packing up our gear and reloading his weapons. He read the look on my face.

"What is it? The girls?" he asked.

I shook my head and sat down on the bed, pulling Jamie down to sit beside me. I held his hands and looked him in the eyes. "They have been giving Ian blood transfusions since we arrived."

Jamie looked confused. "Blood transfusions?"

"I spoke to Dr. Madala. He said Dr. Rostov started Ian on the treatment. The blood . . . James, it's their blood."

I could feel his fingers growing cold. He looked down at the floor. His body, pressed against mine, started shaking.

"I just left him. He's different. I don't know how to explain it. Dr. Madala said Ian is a pet, but Rumor intends to turn him."

"Then we can still save him."

I didn't know what else to say. While I never had a sibling, I understood that it would be useless to try to stop him. Jamie helped people. That was what he did.

"Ian left the infirmary. Wherever he is, I bet Kira and Susan are there," I said.

"Where do you think they are?"

"Fifth floor."

"We can hardly just waltz up there."

"Not unless we'd like to be dinner. But I do have an idea."

Jamie squeezed my hand. "Now, that's my girl."

"I'm guessing you did rope climbing in basic training?"

Jamie looked questioningly at me.

"The dumbwaiter Kiki and I used. There is no way you and I would fit, but we can use the shaft to climb up. From our floor, we can make it . . . I think. Or we could just rappel down the side of the building, but I thought this would provide a bit more subterfuge."

"Layla . . . this is dangerous. They might kill us. Christ, they might eat us. I should go alone. You just get everyone out of here."

I shook my head. "It's no worse than what we've lived through already. I promised Frenchie a long time ago I'd protect those girls. Besides, I don't want to let you have all the fun."

Jamie laughed and started rooting around in his bag. He handed me a pair of gloves and pulled on his as well. "Let's get it over with."

The hallways of the hotel were strangely quiet.

"Where is everyone?" Jamie whispered.

I shook my head.

To our luck, when I lifted the wall hatch on the dumbwaiter, we found it was still lowered to the first floor. Inside, we found the lift system made a ladder we could use to brace ourselves as we climbed up. With a nod, I climbed in and began the ascent. Jamie came after me, closing the hatch behind him. The fifth floor was about twenty feet above. In silence, we climbed.

As we neared the fifth floor, I began to hear voices. People were talking in the hallway outside the dumbwaiter. My hands shook. Could they smell us? Sense us? I closed my eyes and tried to think. When I did, I heard that strange murmuring sound I'd been catching ever since I'd first encountered them. It was like I was almost hearing voices. I'd once read that vampires were telepathic. Was it their telepathy I was hearing? Suddenly, I felt crazy.

Jamie tugged my boot and looked questioningly at me.

I motioned for him to listen.

He nodded.

We waited a moment longer for the voices in the hallway to recede then pressed onward. It was a hard climb. Once we got to the top, I tried to brace myself so I could press the hatch open just a little. Jamie climbed up close to me, and we waited. Everything on the fifth floor seemed very quiet.

With a nod, I pushed the hatch open and peered outside. No one was moving, and it was very dark. There were a few candles lit in the hallway; they turned everything into long shadows. I could see the end of the hall. The window there had been occluded by a large black drape, blocking out even the moonlight.

Despite my earlier boasting, I was afraid. The unthinking undead were one thing, but a calculating vampire who had our girls, who had turned Ian, was something altogether different. Raw violence eats you alive in one big swallow. Intelligent aggression was a slow, painful death.

I pushed the hatch open, slid out, and unsheathed my sword. Jamie exited behind me. I could feel his wild energy around him; he was desperate to save his brother. He held his hunting knife in one hand and a pistol in the other.

We made our way down the hall. Most of the doors were closed. As carefully as possible, I tried a door. It was locked. The hall was exceedingly dark. I could barely make my way in the large expanses of black space between the candles. It was like trying to walk around in a closet—or maybe, a coffin. As we neared a hallway, I motioned to Jamie.

There was an evacuation map that indicated there were three large penthouses at one end of the floor. With a nod, we headed in that direction.

When we turned the corner that housed the penthouses, we saw light emitting from one of the rooms. From inside, we heard voices.

"I thought you said it would be ready," a woman with a heavy accent said. I recognized the voice as belonging to Katya.

"I'm almost done. It's not like pouring wine, you know," I heard Dr. Rostov reply. I heard a strange sound, almost like a grunt. Then there was the awful sound of sliding metal. The doctor spoke again. "Give it maybe fifteen minutes then toss it."

"You're not coming?"

"Later."

We heard a sound like clinking glass headed in our direction.

I pulled Jamie into an alcove. We slid in beside the soda machine. Neither of us dared to breathe. I peered out. In the dim candlelight I saw Katya pass by carrying a large wine decanter and some glasses. The glass decanter caught the candlelight as she passed revealing the shape of a human heart inside. I looked up at Jamie. I could tell by the expression on his face he'd seen it too.

When we no longer heard the glass clinking, we stepped out. From inside the room we heard the doctor groan and heard a strange slurping sound.

We went to the door and looked inside. There we saw the doctor leaning over in a chair, his back to us, a large bundle across his legs. Remembering their ability to turn to shadow, I knew we had to be fast.

I nodded to Jamie and we rushed the room, closing the door behind us. The doctor looked up. His face was dripping with blood. He stood. The body of a young woman dropped to the floor. She had been wearing a pale purple sundress. Her skin looked snow white. The dress strap had been cut. Her chest had been sliced open, her heart removed from her chest. The doctor looked shocked.

"Where are the girls," I whispered harshly, lowering my blade to his throat. He might be able to shift quickly, but not before I could decapitate him.

He smiled at me, but I pressed the blade in more deeply. "Not so fast," I said. "Talk!"

He laughed.

"Talk," I said again in Russian, "you piece of trash. Where are my girls?"

His eyes lit up in surprise. "Ahh, of course," he said with a smile. "They are with her. Go ask her for them," he said with a laugh, his eyes indicating they were in the room at the end of the hall.

"What did you do to my brother?" Jamie cursed at the man through clenched teeth.

"I cured him."

"You condemned him," I corrected.

"Really? Once he has made the final transformation he'll have immortal life in a world where your kind are on a fast track to extinction."

"My kind? I imagine you were once human too, weren't you?" I said

The doctor looked thoughtful, almost as if I reminded him of something he'd long forgotten. For a brief second I saw him remember, and a kind of sadness crossed his face. He then pulled himself together and looked at me with a scolding glance. He looked down at the sword and back at me again. I could see he was calculating.

I shook my head at him.

He smiled.

I swung.

Before he could transform, his head hit the floor, that odd calculating expression on his face. His head rolled across the floor, hitting the girl's lifeless body. Jamie reached down to examine her. Both of her wrists had been slashed open.

"They drained her, took her heart," he said, looking sympathetically at the girl.

I had not seen her before, but she looked to be only a teenager. I eyed the rest of the room. Clearly this was the doctor's blood-letting room. Strange instruments hung from the walls and ceilings. Blood was smeared on the pale yellow fabric of the couches. I shook thinking of Kira and Susan in such a place.

As quietly as possible we did a quick canvas of the room and found it empty. As we were nearing the door again, we heard voices in the hallway.

"Where is Rostov?" I heard Rumor ask.

My heart skipped a beat.

"Door is closed. He must have gone down already," I heard Finn reply.

She sighed heavily. "Bring them," she instructed someone.

In the hallway, I heard the muffled cries of Kira and Susan. I reached for the door, but Jamie stopped me.

"Not yet," he mouthed to me.

From the hallway, I heard a door click open and the sound of Rumor's receding voice. The sound of footsteps drifted upward and away.

"Roof?" Jamie questioned.

I nodded.

We waited a few more minutes and then slowly opened the door. The hallway was still dark, but the door to Rumor's penthouse was now open. We were about to follow the stairs to the roof when we heard noise coming from inside her room. Turning back, we moved slowly into the penthouse.

Clearly, this was Rumor's space. The penthouse was the most lavishly furnished of all the places I'd seen in the hotel. On top of that, it looked like

Rumor had brought along artifacts from her former life with her. Portraits of Rumor hinted that she was much older than her contemporary name suggested. There were images of her in a white wig which dated to the late 1700s and other paintings that indicated some sort of French connection. Smaller paintings showed her in medieval dress. Figurines, matryoshka dolls, and paintings with a phoenix, bears, and Baba Yaga images revealed her Slavic roots. Again, however, we heard the strange sound; it sounded like thrashing and heavy breathing. We followed the noise to a side bedroom where we saw movement on the bed.

Jamie pulled his LED flashlight from his vest and motioned to me; I got ready. He clicked the light on to reveal a single body lying in the bed covered with a sheet. It stirred. My heart raced. I positioned the sword and moved toward the bed. Grabbing the end of the sheet, I pulled it off. There, strapped to the bed, lay one of the undead. It turned, jerking, toward the light, straining at its restraints.

"What the hell is she doing with that?" Jamie whispered.

I looked at it. It had once been human, a male with long, dark hair. His skin was only slightly wilted. He had tattoos on both arms. He hissed and bit at us.

Set me free, a voice said in my head.

"Did you hear that?" I asked Jamie.

"Hear what?"

Set me free or kill me.

I stared at the undead man. His moon-white eyes looked right at me. He'd gone still. It was like he was waiting. My god! Had I really heard him?

I lifted my sword and stabbed the creature between the eyes. The spark behind those white, undead eyes flickered out.

Then we heard movement in the outer foyer. Jamie clicked off the light. We were trapped. There was nowhere to hide. A second later, Ian's familiar shape appeared in the candle-lit outer room.

Jamie moved forward. I tried to pull him back, but he moved before I could grab him.

"Ian?" Jamie called quietly.

What had once been Ian looked at his brother. From behind, I could see Jamie's body stiffen as he took it in. Ian stood staring at Jamie.

"I can smell you, Layla," Ian said after a moment.

I came out of the shadow and stood behind Jamie. My sword was lowered but my hold on the grip was tight.

Ian stared at the two of us. Then, he turned to go.

"What will you do, just stand aside and let them drain Kira and Susan?" Jamie called, taking a few steps after his brother.

Ian stopped in the doorway. He looked back over his shoulder at Jamie. Ian gazed at his brother for a moment then walked back into the dark hallway. Jamie and I stood in the darkness.

"That was not my brother," Jamie whispered.

"I--" I started, but I didn't know what to say. I'm sorry didn't feel like enough. I was sorry, but it was too late for Ian. Jamie knew that now. "Kira and Susan are still alive."

Jamie seemed to come back to himself. He looked down at me and took a deep breath. After a moment, he nodded, and we went forward. We found the door that led to the roof. Opening it as quietly as possible, we entered the stairwell. Carefully, we climbed, expecting to be greeted by a host of vampires partying on the roof. Instead, we emerged in the moonlight to find no one. It was completely empty.

Jamie and I stood on the roof and gazed at the grounds of the HarpWind. The night was nearly cloudless. Silver stars, uncorrupted by city lights, filled the sky. The Milky Way illuminated the skyline, the crescent moon hanging like an ornament. It must have been sometime after midnight. I went to the edge of the roof and looked over.

Below, we saw hotel staff coming out of the back of the hotel and heading toward the western end of the island. They were laughing and joking, their voices rising upward. Several minutes later, Corbin, Finn, Matilda, and Katya appeared. They too made their way west across the lawns. Following behind them was Rumor. She had on a gauzy red dress. It blew all around her in the wind. Holding her hand was Susan who held fast to Kira. Anger nearly boiled over in me. They walked across the lawn and into a thicket of trees, disappearing into the shadow of the night.

"How did they get down?" Jamie wondered.

"As shadows or maybe jumped. They seem to have enhanced physical skill and strength."

We turned and headed back inside. We'd have to take the stairs if we wanted to follow them. When we pushed open the door to the fifth floor hallway, we saw that the door to Rostov's room was open. We were found out. A moment later, a woman appeared in the doorframe. I recognized her at once. It was the same vampire who'd tried to assassinate me.

"This time, you're mine," she said and lunged at me. She grabbed me by the throat and slammed me against the wall, suspending me several feet up. Her strong hands squeezed my neck. I rasped. Jamie plunged his knife into the back of her neck. She turned her head for a moment and gave him an annoyed expression. When she did so, I took my chance. I reached into the pocket of my vest and pulled out the holy water. Flicking out the cork, I opened it. She turned at me and grinned. I splashed the water onto her face.

She dropped me at once and let out a howl, her hands covering her face. Her skin smoked with a strange sulfur-like burning smell. She moved her hands for just a moment. I saw a horrid sight. It looked as if her skin was melting from her bones. She fell over; her body burnt to a pile of ash.

Jamie grabbed my hand. "Come on! Someone could have heard her."

We ran down the hall and took the stairs to the fourth floor.

"We can't wait for dawn. We need to get everyone out of here now. I'll go for the girls. Get everyone gathered at the east end of the hotel. Once I have the girls I'll meet you there."

"No. We can go together."

"There's no time!"

"But what if something happens to you?"

"Go to the eastern end of Enita Island, to the shoreline. There is another, smaller island just off shore. There's a boat there. Take everyone to the other island. It is a place of safety. At the center of the island is a stone labyrinth. Follow it to completion. It will take you off the island."

Jamie looked amazed. "How do you know that?"

"A fox told me."

"Layla?"

"A kind of spirit, a fox woman, guided me there and told me the labyrinth is a doorway."

"To where?"

"Out of here."

"I thought foxes were supposed to be tricksters," he said absently, but then added. "I suppose it would just be too easy to take the yacht?"

"They can transform into shadow. They could find us if we take the yacht."

"Yep, too easy."

"We'll be fine. I'll get the girls and meet you there."

"Layla," Jamie said grabbing me and pulling me close. "I love you," he whispered and gave me a deep kiss. "Please, be careful."

"I love you too," I replied, and squeezed his chin, kissing him sweetly. "Hey, we survived hundreds of the undead so far, what's a handful of vampires?"

Jamie shook his head at me. "See you soon."

"See you soon." And we set off in different directions.

CHAPTER 32

THE HOTEL WAS DEAD. IT was too late for any survivors to still be up, and all of the staff was gone. Apparently they had gone to the party Ian had mentioned. The idea that it was a party worried me. What were they celebrating, and what, besides that poor girl's heart in a jar, was on the menu? I shuddered to consider it.

I exited the hotel. Hiding in the shadows as much as possible, I went west. I took the path I'd seen Rumor and her entourage take into the thick forest. The air was cool under the trees. They made a thick canopy which nearly occluded the moonlight. I stepped carefully through the woods trying to make as little sound as possible. The earthy woods smell was tangy and sweet. I passed through the woods, worrying every shadow was one of them, and soon found myself at the edge of a very large pond. On the other side was a reception hall. Through the nearly floor to ceiling windows, I could see people moving around. At such a distance, however, they were merely shapes. The room was full of candle-light; the flames bounced on the waters of the pond outside. Apparently, I'd found the party.

I kept low and near the water's edge. When I neared the building, I heard the outside door open and close, but no one came toward me. The sound of happy and excited voices filled the night air when the door opened. When I was finally near the hall, I lay on my belly, snuck up the bankside, and looked inside.

I wasn't sure if what I saw within was a blood bath or an orgy. I squelched the scream that nearly escaped my lips. Inside, almost everyone was either naked or half undressed. The hosts were drinking the blood of those I'd see during the day, the pets. White flesh was streaked red with dripping blood. Many were having sex and being bled at the same time, sometimes being eaten by more than one vampire. From the looks on their faces, they were in a state of rapture. My eyes scanned the room for Kira and Susan, praying they were not witness to such a horrific sight, praying they were not being eaten alive. As I scanned, my eyes fell on Ian. He and Rumor were lost in their own ecstasy; he was thrusting into her while she bit his shoulder, her legs wrapped around his waist, blood dripping down his back. I felt myself tear up but forced the emotions away. I didn't have time to feel the pain. I couldn't let it in just then. It was too horrible, and

Kira and Susan still needed me. I stood and maneuvered toward the back of the building.

Once I got to the side of the building, I looked into the window of one of the back rooms. Kira and Susan were sitting side by side on the floor in the kitchen. They had been redressed in simple white gowns, their hair adorned with spring flowers. They were holding fast to each other and looked scared, but they were alive. Carefully, I tried the window. It was locked. But there was a door at the back that led directly to the kitchen.

I slid around the side of the building. There was no one there, and the door was ajar. I opened it. Kira and Susan looked up. They were both startled to see me. Kira opened her mouth to call out, but Susan quickly covered her mouth. I put my finger over my lips and motioned them to come to me.

Quietly, the two girls came hand in hand. I led them out. As I turned to look for an escape route, I found myself face to face with Corbin.

He smiled menacingly at me, and this time I could see his fangs. "I told you to remember that you asked to come."

In a heartbeat, I dropped Susan's hand, freed the shashka from the scabbard across my back, and let it sing through the air. With one fell swoop, I sliced off Corbin's head. It hit the earth with a thud. The creature's ridiculous smile was still on his face.

"Shut up," I said and kicked the head into the weeds. I then slid the body under a thicket.

The noise didn't seem to attract anyone. I grabbed the girls, carrying Susan and holding on to Kira, and we took off in a run toward the hotel.

We had almost passed through the forest when my hands started to tingle. There was someone in the forest with us. I stopped and looked around. The moonlight above cast long shadows everywhere. I swore I saw something moving but could not get a fix. My eyes darted around trying to spot one of them, but I saw nothing clearly.

"What's wrong?" Kira whispered.

I put my finger to my lip to silence her. I bent to pick her up, but in that same moment I felt someone behind me. There was a strange feeling of built up energy when he morphed from shadow to corporeal form. The leaves crackled under its feet.

"Going somewhere?" a male voice asked.

I turned to see Ambrosio standing there.

"Go away," Susan yelled at him. I felt a tug on my vest and then Ambrosio flung backward, a look of shock and pain on his face. He opened his mouth to scream but fell into a pile of ash.

I looked at Susan. She had pulled the water gun Jamie had given me from my vest. She'd blasted him with holy water.

"Nice shooting," I told her, and then hoisting up Kira, I set off in a run.

I ran across the lawn toward the eastern end of the hotel. Everyone was waiting. When they spotted me, Jamie and Frenchie rushed to intercept me. I set the girls down. They ran to their mother.

Jamie wrapped his arm around me and kissed the top of my head. "Amazing," he whispered.

Frenchie smiled at me as she kissed her daughters. I saw her eye their clothes, and she too could guess the meaning of such dress.

"We're in trouble. We need to go, now," I replied.

"Oh, Layla, thank god. Where did you find those girls?" Ethel asked.

"Don't ask," I replied. "We need to move."

"Where is Ian?" Mrs. Finch asked.

I gazed at Jamie who said nothing. I shook my head.

"What should we do?" Larry asked.

"We need to take out the hotel and the yacht," I instructed. "Jeff, you got the bottles?"

He nodded, tapping some boxes with his foot.

"What is going on here?" one of the survivors asked.

"Just stay with Layla," Ethel replied.

"We have the cloth strips," Summer said and handed them to me.

"Quickly, start corking bottles," I instructed.

"Molotovs?" Kiki asked.

I nodded. Jeff and the others started rapidly corking vodka bottles with strips of cloth. I could imagine my grandmother shaking her head—a terrible waste.

"We can take out the hotel," Tom said, and several others around him nodded.

"What about the yacht? Won't we need it?" Kiki asked.

"No, everyone needs to come with me. There is another way off the island. We have to go to a smaller island just off shore. There," I said, pointing toward the shoreline where the fox had led me down the earthen steps earlier that day.

"We got the yacht," Jeff said as he and Gary packed a bag of liquor bottles.

"Guys, we need to haul ass. We've already killed some of them. They could be on us at any minute. Fire. Decapitation. I don't think guns will do anything," I cautioned.

Moments later, everyone was moving off in different directions. Jamie headed out with Tom and his group. I led my group through the rocky weeds down to the shoreline. The moon above illuminated the waves. The rowboat was where I had left it.

"Quickly," I said, motioning them toward the boat.

I turned to Larry. "Get everyone on that island as fast as possible."

"On it, Layla."

I grabbed Larry's arm. "Frenchie and the girls on the first trip."

He nodded affirmatively.

I waited until he got the first boat loaded and was headed safely across the waves. Then I ran back toward the hotel. Just as I reached the lawn, I heard the sound of breaking glass and a familiar boom as fire exploded. The burning alcohol sprayed across the wooden thatches.

From the western end traveling east, I saw explosion after explosion tearing at the side of the hotel. In the firelight, I saw Jamie's and Tom's hustling figures.

Then I heard another sound. A wailing, like a banshee scream, sounded from somewhere in the distance.

I saw Tom and Jamie stop for a moment then set off in a sprint across the lawn.

Then there was another explosion from the direction of the dock. The yacht was on fire.

My heart raced. I melded back into the grass and watched: Jamie, Tom, Will, Dusty, Buddie, and Mr. Jones raced across the lawn toward me.

A shadow moved across the night's sky. There was another scream as the creatures spotted the men.

"Move!" I screamed at them.

In a heartbeat, two of the vampires were amongst us. They moved too fast.

Jamie dodged one. It was Finn. Jamie shot at him. Finn dodged the bullets and lunged at Jamie. Jamie slid to the ground, under and behind the vampire.

I ran toward them. Grabbing the last vial of holy water from my vest, I rushed the creature.

When Finn caught sight of me, he went in for the kill.

I unstopped the liquid and just as Finn was about to grab me, I rained holy water across his face.

He screeched a horrific cry, clutching his face. He melted into the ground, crumbling into a heap of ash.

Then I heard Mr. Jones scream. Matilda had grabbed him. She hovered about ten feet in the air, snapped his neck, and dropped him.

Next, she made a move toward Buddie who shot an arrow through her throat. It slowed her. She stopped to pull it out, an annoyed expression on her face.

Will swept in behind her. Lighting one of the liquor bottles, he pitched it at her. Before she had time to react, it exploded, raining fire all over her. She wailed in agony.

I looked up. More shadowed figures moved across the horizon.

"Now, now, let's go," I screamed. We took off through the weeds. Down we went through the brush and onto the marsh. We rushed through the swampy water to the stone-lined shore.

Larry had the last of the survivors rowed halfway to the island.

"We're fucked," Will said.

"We have to get to the island. They can't touch us there. Go, go, swim," I yelled at them.

"What about you?" Dusty asked.

"Jeff and Gary are still out there."

"Layla, go, you're the only one who really knows what to do," Jamie said.

Just then, the shadowy shapes of Rumor and Katya appeared near the hotel. They were scanning for us.

"Go, go, let's go," Jamie said and pulled me toward the water.

"But--"

"Now, Layla, move your ass," Buddie said.

We went crashing into the water. It was bitterly cold. I could feel the heavy weight of my equipment on me and suddenly I worried I might not make it. Adrenaline pushing me forward, I forced myself to swim. The boat was just nearing the shoreline. As I swam, I saw Larry unload the rest of the people and hustle them up the bank. In the darkness, I saw the shadowed crowd watching the events unfold in horror. I could not imagine the sight: the hotel burning, the other survivors swimming, the vampires hunting.

As I emerged from the water, I heard an ear-piercing scream. Rumor had spotted us. Dusty and Will helped me stand. We turned. In full flight, Katya and Rumor darted over the water. At the same moment, Jeff and Gary crashed through the marshy brush onto the shore of Enita Island. Not seeing the vampires, Jeff called out.

"Layla," he screamed.

Rumor turned and in the blink of an eye, she fell upon him. She smashed him under her foot like a fly. She reached down, plucking his head off, and drank blood from the trunk of his neck. She then threw the bloody head across the water to me.

Jeff's head rolled across the beach, his agape mouth and wide eyes staring at me.

Katya grabbed Gary. Twisting his neck, she sank her fangs into him.

Jamie and Buddie emerged from the water. We all turned toward the bankside.

"Don't look, just go," I said.

"Ah, Ms. Katana, you forgot someone, no?" Rumor called to me.

I turned back. Out of nowhere, Ian was standing beside Rumor.

Jamie stopped. He turned and took two steps back toward the water.

The HarpWind was completely engulfed in flame. Orange light began to fill the night's sky.

Rumor then took Ian by the waist and they hovered across the water coming to land just inches off shore.

"What is this place?" Ian asked her.

"Sun island. Don't take another step ashore. It will burn you alive," Rumor replied. She, however, was much bolder. "You come here and burn my house, do you," she said to me as she took a step toward the island.

I drew my sword.

She looked at it and then at me. "And you lie as well," she added, switching to dialect.

"If I must," I replied in Russian, "but I didn't come looking for trouble. You did."

"Eh," she said with a shrug, "one must eat."

She was just out of my reach, and she knew it. She was baiting me, and I knew it.

I looked at Ian. He stood in the water watching us. I could not read his expression.

Realizing at last that I would not take the bait, she lunged at me.

I stepped back deeper onto the shoreline. It did not seem to faze her. She crashed hard into me, knocking my sword from my hand. I saw it shine just once in the moonlight then fall into the water.

She was unbelievably strong. I fell. She grabbed me by the boot and pulled me back into the water.

Jamie lunged at her. She let go of me, moving to defend herself, and knocked him back. He flew several feet and crashed onto the rocks. Dusty rushed forward and pulled him back toward the bank. It looked like he was unconscious. I heard an arrow whoosh overhead. It caught Rumor in the shoulder.

She paused. In that moment I bounced back onto my feet and pulled the poyasni doe- and wolf-headed daggers from my boots. She pulled the arrow from her shoulder and lunged at me. I dodged her advance and took a swipe at her. It connected; I slashed a long line across her face. Blood dripped from the wound for a moment then healed itself. She smiled at me and lunged again. I bounced back closer toward the shore. Rumor pursued me, but her feet had begun to smolder. She jumped, pushing me sideways, knocking me into the waves, knocking us both away from the island.

I rebalanced myself and lunged again, this time cutting a thin line across her throat. It was a close cut, but I had not hit home. Enraged, she came at me. She crashed into me. I fell backward, underwater. The water rushed over my face. My head hit a rock on the lake bottom. I struggled but could not move. I opened my eyes but saw only black waves. I could feel the weight of her hands on my neck, her knee on my chest. I tried to push her off but could not.

307

I heard the sound of gunfire, but she seemed unfazed.

My eyes fluttered closed. In a fragment of a second, I saw my grandmother smile at me. The next second, I felt Rumor's hands release from my neck, and I was pulled from the water. Someone lifted me and carried me back to the shore, setting me down gently. I coughed hard, spitting out the lake water, and sat up, opening my eyes.

Ian stood over me, my shashka in his hand. Rumor's body, her red dress fanning all around her, floated, decapitated, in the water. Her head lay on the shoreline. It flickered then burnt into a pile of ash.

Katya shrieked then fled.

Ian handed my sword to me. He looked back at Jamie who lay unconscious then turned again to me. He smiled softly. For a moment, I saw the old Ian in his eyes. Then he burst into flame. I reached toward him, but within seconds, Ian was gone.

Moments later, Buddie and Dusty pulled me, half-drowned and in a state of shock, onto the bank. Jamie was just coming around to consciousness; he was leaning between Will and Larry. At the inferno that was now the HarpWind above us, we heard the shrieking sounds of the remaining vampires. I pulled myself together and went to the front of the group.

"This way," I said and led them to the far side of the island.

The moonlight barely illuminated our path in the dark, but when we came to stand above the labyrinth, a strange glow filled the place. The rocks which had seemed so mundane in the light of day had an eerie blue hue. The labyrinth's snake effigy form glowed.

"What is this place?" Summer asked.

"A doorway," I replied.

"To where?" Frenchie asked.

"Anywhere but here," I said. I led them down the stairs and into the labyrinth. We turned around and around the labyrinth until we reached the middle.

"Follow it to its end," I said. "The gateway should be open."

Everyone looked scared. Buddie nodded at me and took the lead. One by one, they traced the spiraling stones. As each reached the middle, they simply shimmered then disappeared. Jamie paused before he passed through. I nodded to him, and he took the final steps, disappearing. Once they had all gone, I paused. Smoke billowed on the horizon, fingers of fire trailing up into the night's sky. It cast a haze on the moon. I took a deep breathe. Following the serpent's tongue, I too passed through the gateway to a new world.

I hope you enjoyed *The Harvesting*. If so, please consider telling your friends or posting a short review. Word of mouth is an author's best friend!

If you would like updates about this series, information about new releases, and free short stories, please join my mailing list:
http://eepurl.com/OSPDH

Thank you!

Acknowledgements

With special thanks to Michael Hall Jr., Susan Houts, José Otero, Naomi Clewett, and Catherine Amick

About the Author

Melanie Karsak grew up in rural northwestern Pennsylvania and earned a Master's degree in English from Gannon University. A steampunk connoisseur, white elephant collector, and zombie whisperer, the author currently lives in Florida with her husband and two children. She is an Instructor of English at Eastern Florida State College.

Keep in touch with the author online. She's really nice!

Blog: melaniekarsak.blogspot.com
Twitter: www.twitter.com/melaniekarsak
Email: melanie@clockpunkpress.com
Facebook: www.facebook.com/authormelaniekarsak
Pinterest: www.pinterest.com/melaniekarsak
I'm a Goodreads author!

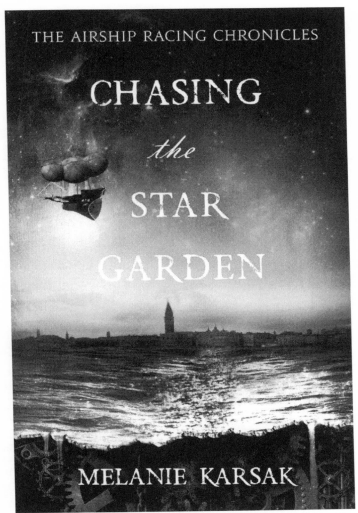

THE AIRSHIP RACING CHRONICLES

CHASING

the

STAR

GARDEN

MELANIE KARSAK

Join Melanie Karsak for an exciting steampunk romantic adventure series in Chasing the Star Garden.

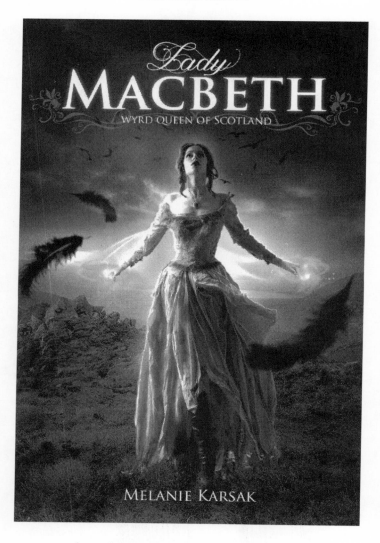

Something wicked this way comes . . .
Meet the real Lady Macbeth, Summer 2014!

91105375R00193

Made in the USA
Columbia, SC
16 March 2018